Sweater Girls

Sweater Girls

AMBER MALONE

To my best friend who happens to be my husband, Anthony. To my children who listened to this story every day and shared valuable feedback! To my mom and my dad who encouraged me to share with the world and believed in me and to all my friends and family, thank you for helping me bring my dream to reality. I am so blessed! Love you guys!

Memory Verse 1

I know something's wrong. On the way home from school, Mom and I stopped for fast food and Mom let me order whatever I wanted. I ordered the Super-Mega burrito that has a hot dog and barbecue chips inside and chili cheese fries on top. Then, when the lady in the drive-thru asked if I wanted to try the new cinnamon rolls, not only did Mom let me order two cinnamon rolls, she also said I could have the iced coffee. For the record, on any normal day I'm not even allowed to drink coffee.

Emily, my favorite doll, is sitting in Mom's reading chair in my room when Mom comes to tuck me in. Emily has curly hair like me; she's wearing a pink dress with red roses and pink shoes. Mom sits on my bed. She says she has some very sad news: she lost her job yesterday.

"It'll be okay, Mom," I say, rubbing her back.

"I just don't know what we're going to do," Mom looks sadder than I've ever seen her.

"God has a plan," I say. That's what Ms. Bethany, my small group leader at church told us last week when a kid asked if God could see his future. Every week, Ms. Bethany teaches us a new memory verse, which I always memorize because if I know the previous week's memory verse by heart, I get to pick a prize. I usually pick a new bracelet. I collect them.

Mom lifts her head. She's breathing in and out the way you do when the doctor listens to your heart. One of her eyebrows is higher than the other one. "I'd sure like to know what that plan is," she sniffs. She wipes her nose with the back of her fingers and clears the frog in her throat. "I want you to stay home tomorrow." I can feel the muscles in my body tying themselves into double knots.

"Why?" I whine. I *have* to go to school. Tera Mulligan, the meanest girl in my class, invited me to meet her on the blacktop. She used to make fun of me all the time, but ever since I found her favorite gold heart locket underneath the desks in our class, she's started being nice to me. Plus, it's Fun Day Friday and we always watch a movie or play a game like Heads Up Seven Up or Four Corners.

"I have to run some errands, and I can't do that if have to pick you up," Mom rubs her forehead.

"But—I can go to Safe Zone."

"Not now, Joanna, please," she snaps.

"Am I going back on Monday?" Mom closes her eyes and pinches the top of her nose with her thumb and pointer finger.

"So I might never go back?" I'm breathing fast, like I'm racing across the entire P.E. field.

"Joanna! Stop! O-kaaaaay? Of course you're going

2

back!" Mom chops the air with her hand. Emily is staring at me with her arms spread out like the Scarecrow in the Wizard of Oz. Mom gives me a kiss on my forehead and tucks my puffy pink blanket under my chin. "Get some sleep, ladybug."

"No story?" I ask as she walks to the doorway.

"Not tonight." She rubs her eyes again. Mom is forgetting that Emily is afraid of the dark and I can't sleep when Emily is scared.

"Night," I say. As Mom closes the door, I grab Emily so she doesn't feel lost in the darkness.

"Don't worry Emily, I won't let it get you," I say, but it's too late. I can hear the tornado coming for us. It sounds like an enormous waterfall, making me shake all over. I pray and ask God to keep us safe and help Mom find a job, because if the tornado gets Mom, I won't have anyone left.

Memory Verse 2

Luke 6:31

"Do for others what you want them to do for you."

It's 6:30 a.m., time to get up for school. Usually Mom drags me out of bed. It's not that I don't like school, but I would much rather go roller-skating, or watch one of my favorite shows.

"Yes ma'am," Mom says. Her voice sounds happy, but not exactly normal. She puts down the phone. "Get in the shower, brush your teeth, and get dressed, I'll be back to do your hair. You know the drill." She's already dressed in her work clothes, a black skirt and a black and white polka-dot blouse.

"Did you get a job already?" Wow, God, that was fast.

"I'm going to a job fair today," she says.

"What's a job fair?" I picture Mom at a fair with her boss and her coworkers, eating candied apples at the top of a Ferris wheel.

"A job fair is where people who are looking for a job can meet possible employers. I'm going to bring my resume and talk to companies that are looking for new employees."

"What's a resume? It sounds like an expensive dessert." I imagine Mom sitting in a fancy restaurant. A waiter with a curly black mustache and a long twisty beard is holding a silver platter with a glass bowl of resume. He says, with an accent like Alfred from Batman, (ahem) "Excuse me, ma'am, your resume is here."

"It's a document that explains my work experience and qualifications for a job," Mom says, popping my thought bubble.

"That sounds nothing like dessert."

"Let's get your hair done, ladybug; I want to get there early." Mom peeks at her cell phone. I'm moving faster than I ever have in my entire ten years on the planet.

"I wish you were always this motivated," she says.

"Wanna play a game?" I ask as Mom gathers my curls with both hands.

"Smure!" she says with my ponytail holder in her mouth. I've learned to understand Mom when she talks around my hair clips or ponytail holders.

"Okay, I'll say, 'I'm going on a trip and I'm taking apples,' for example, because apples start with the letter A, and then you have to think of something to take that starts with the next letter in the alphabet." Mom nods, wrapping the ponytail holder twice around my hair. "Oh, and you can't say the same thing I said because you can't take something on the trip twice," I add.

"Got it," she smiles. It's nice to see Mom smiling again.

"Okay I'll start. I'm going on a trip and I'm taking an aardvark."

"That's a good one... I'm going on a trip and I'm taking a beach."

"Mom, you can't take a whole beach."

"Why not?" She frowns. "I could really use a trip to the beach right now."

5

"Why don't we go?" I ask. We're only a four-hour drive from California. Mom and I visit the San Diego beach all the time so I can add more seashells to my collection.

"I wish we could, ladybug, but right now isn't the best time."

"I know, we don't have enough money," I sigh. Mom takes a deep breath as she kneels down to meet my eyes.

"I don't want you worrying about money. I'm sorry about last night. I never should have put you in that position." She cups my face in her hands.

"It's okay," I say.

Mom shakes her head. "No, it's not, but it's your turn." She pushes my nose like a doorbell.

"I'm going on a trip and I'm taking a camel. Camels can travel really long distances, and did you know some people call camels the 'ships of the desert' because they can also carry a lot of weight? I could bring a lot of stuff."

"Wow, you really know your animals, don't you?" Mom ties a blue ribbon in my hair.

"Yup, that's why I want to be a veterinarian. I want to learn as much as I can about animals. Your turn."

"Hmmm—I'm going on a trip and I'm taking a dolphin," Mom says.

"I'm going on a trip and I'm taking earwax," I laugh.

"That's pretty gross, Joanna."

"Not really, earwax is good for you. If it wasn't for earwax, your ears would be dry and itchy."

"Interesting," Mom says. "Do you wanna bring your lunch or eat a hot lunch today?" Fridays are pizza days so I don't want to bring my lunch.

"Definitely a hot lunch."

"Grab your backpack and get your shoes on." Since it's so early and school doesn't start until 8:30, I'm going to Safe Zone. That's where kids can hang out before and after school in the cafeteria. I love going to Safe Zone because I can play games and I have a lot of friends there. Safe Zone has the best cinnamon rolls—they're filled with creamy white sugary icing. Whenever Mom makes cinnamon rolls, she only adds a dot of sugar-free icing.

I say goodbye to Emily and head to the car. The wind blows my ponytail around, slapping my cheeks. The cold air makes my lips feel chapped. I zip up my purple sweater over my white T-shirt. I'm glad I wore jeans today. Mom hugs her arms as she runs to our car.

"Wow, I should have brought a jacket." She shivers.

"Do you want me to run in and grab it?"

"That would be great honey, thanks." She hands me the keys. The wind pushes me backwards as I struggle to get to the front door. Inside, Mom's black leather jacket is lying on her bed. When I pick it up from the bed, a white paper with big red letters falls to the floor. It's a bill from the power company and it says: PAST DUE FINAL DISCONNECT NOTICE. I guess Mom must have wanted to bring it with her. I check five times to make sure the front door is locked. Mom honks the horn as I'm running to the car. It's so warm and toasty the windows are fogging.

"I brought this," I say, handing Mom the bill. Her smile turns upside down. She puts the bill in the glove compartment, then wipes her cheeks, blinking fast. If Mom doesn't pay the bill, we won't have power and we'll be in the dark all the time. We don't even have candles or a flashlight. What would Emily do? I should have brought Emily with me. She could have hidden in my backpack.

At Safe Zone, I sit down with my friends Kelly and Tiffany. They're playing my favorite game, Apples to Apples.

"Can I play the next game?" I ask.

"You can play this game if you want—we just started," Kelly says. I look over at Mom talking to the Safe Zone teacher, Ms. Sims. Ms. Sims is shaking her head and pointing to the computer screen.

"I'm sorry," she says. Mom lowers her head.

"I'm sure I paid for the week," she says, loudly enough that the whole room can hear.

"Joanna, it's your turn," Kelly says.

"Can't she stay today?" Mom cries.

"Why is your mom crying?" Tiffany asks. My face is so hot I wish I was invisible!

"C'mon Joanna!" Mom calls me with her pointer finger. Ms. Sims tells Mom to wait a minute and disappears into the "staff only" room. When she comes back, she says something to Mom.

"Thank you so much," Mom says, giving Ms. Sims a hug. I don't know if I should sit down yet, so I keep standing.

"Have a good day, ladybug!" Mom waves. I wave goodbye as the bell rings. Suddenly I remember that I was supposed to meet Tera on the blacktop. I'm the last to join our class line. Tera and Riley are laughing about something up front. Tera notices me staring, so I wave to her. She smiles at me and waves back. Mrs. Washington waits for the line to settle down before we walk to our classroom.

"Come up here," Tera says, but Mrs. Washington gives me the look that my Mom gives me right before she says, "You'd better not." Tera and Riley are best friends. They both have really nice clothes and shoes, and Tera has diamond earrings. Tera is wearing a jean jacket with green shorts folded above her knees and brown sandals, even though it's freezing cold, and Riley is wearing overall jean shorts with a pink shirt underneath and white sandals; it's amazing they haven't turned into human ice cubes.

Inside our classroom, our desks look totally different. Instead of being in groups of four they are now arranged into L-shaped rows around the room.

"Why are our desks moved around?" Tera asks.

"Everybody settle down. You'll notice I've made some changes. Some of you have struggled with working together in your groups silently," Mrs. Washington says. The whole class groans.

I find my name card next to Tera's. My stomach hurts.

"Looks like we're neighbors," Tera says.

"Sorry I didn't meet you at the blacktop. I had to go to Safe Zone," I say. Tera is giving me a confused look. She hands me a white envelope. I don't think she remembers we were supposed to meet on the blacktop.

"This weekend is my birthday. I'm having a swim party—wanna come?" Tera asks.

"But it's so cold," I say.

"No it's not, it's gonna be sixty degrees," she snaps.

"Okay, sure," I say, even though Mom will probably say no.

"Wear your bikini and bring sunglasses, I have towels." Bikini? I don't even have a one-piece that fits me.

"Thanks for inviting me." I put the invitation in my backpack. Tera shrugs her shoulders.

"O-kay," she says, letting me know how weird it was that I thanked her for inviting me. My friend Megan is watching me open my invitation. I know Tera didn't invite Megan because she doesn't like Megan, which should make me feel horrible since two weeks ago Tera didn't like me, but this week she does and I feel like I won the "cool" award and the whole school is cheering for me. Riley's sitting behind Megan and she's pointing her finger in her mouth making the "gag" face. Tera's poking me and giggling so I'm giggling a little too.

"Look at dirty Megan with her dirty shoes," Tera whispers through her teeth so Mrs. Washington won't hear. I'm smiling, but only because Megan's not looking.

"She smells so bad, I can't believe you were friends with her," Tera whispers.

"Good morning, students," Mr. Suarez, our principal, says through the intercom. It's time for the morning announcements. I'm glad Tera's stopped talking about Megan. I look at Megan and she's looking back at me. I know what she's thinking, because I'm thinking the same thing about myself.

Memory Verse 3

1 Corinthians 13:7

"Love never gives up on people. It never stops trusting,
never loses hope, and never quits."

It's lunchtime. I'm sitting with Tera and Riley, but all I can think about is how I used to sit with Megan.

"Wanna dress the same on Monday?" Tera asks.

"Sure," I say, taking my eyes off Megan sitting by herself. Tera flips her light-brown hair behind her and Riley does the same with her black cornrows.

"I'm wearing black shorts and my black high-top Converse," Tera says.

"Okay, I'll wear black shorts too," Riley says, reapplying her lip gloss. The good news is, I have black shorts. The bad news is, Mom will never let me wear shorts with it being so cold outside.

"Me too," I hear myself say. *You could always change at school*, I tell myself, feeling a twinge of guilt. Megan has barely touched her pizza.

"Are you on Screen Chat?" Tera pulls out her cell phone.

"No," I say, dreading the next question. Mom thinks I'm too young to have a cell phone even though practically all the girls in my class have one.

"You should join. My user name is TeraBeara21, and

Riley, I forgot yours—tell Joanna your username." Riley has the newest smartphone with a diamond-studded case.

"It's Supergirl4321," she says.

"Take out your phone, Jo—I'll show you the app," Tera says casually. The only person who's ever called me "Jo" was my dad, before he died in a motorcycle accident when I was six. My mouth feels dry, my head hurts, and I want to crawl under the table.

"I left my phone at home," I mumble.

"What's your number? I'll save it in my phone and text you mine," Tera says.

"I'll be right back. I have to use the bathroom," I say. Tera and Riley are lost in their cell phones as I walk past Megan and tap her shoulder. She looks at her shoulder like a spider's crawling on it.

"Meet me in the bathroom," I say. I don't know if she'll come or not, but I have to talk to her without Tera and Riley around. The bathroom stinks, and there's balled-up toilet paper scattered all over the floor. The mirror is coated with fingerprints, old green gum, and an unknown brown substance. Megan walks in and I feel like I just got off a rollercoaster after eating a tub of ice cream.

"Hey," I say.

"Hey," she says back.

"Are you okay?" Megan gives me a look like she ate a mouthful of lima beans and liver.

"Yeah, why?"

"I don't know—I know we always sit together, but Tera and Riley asked me to sit with them." It sounds even worse

12

saying it out loud. Megan pushes her cheeks into a grin. Her dimples show, and her brown eyes sparkle.

"It's okay," she says.

"So you're *not* mad at me?"

"No." She shakes her head while shrugging one shoulder. Even though Megan says she's not mad at me, it only makes me feel worse because she should be. If Megan said, *"Yes Joanna, I'm really mad at you for making fun of me when we're supposed to be friends and ditching me for Tera when she always used to make fun of you,"* then I would feel better because I could say, *"You're right, I'm sorry."* I suppose I could say "sorry" without her telling me what she should be telling me, but then I would have to admit I was making fun of her when it seems like she doesn't even know. How could she not know? It was pretty obvious. She *has* to know, but if she knows then why is she being so nice to me?

"So…" I say, peeling my fingernails. "This morning you weren't mad at me either?" The bell rings. Megan jumps; the bell is much louder in the bathroom.

"We'd better go," she says. I follow Megan out of the bathroom and search for Tera and Riley. They've emptied my tray for me and thrown away my chocolate milk. Tera is calling me, but I want to stay with Megan. I need to make sure we're still friends.

"I think they want you to line up with them," Megan says.

Tera looks like a cheerleader jumping up and down, "Joanna c'mon! C'mon! Let's go!" she cheers.

"Yeah, I should probably go. Sorry." I raise my

eyebrows.

"It's okay," Megan says. Why does she have to be so nice when she knows I'm being so mean to her? I run over to Tera and Riley. Tera hooks her arm in mine and I link my other arm with Riley.

"I can't wait till tomorrow, It's gonna be awesome and Jake's gonna be there," Tera giggles. Tera hadn't said anything about boys being there. I blow out air louder than I mean to.

"What's wrong, Jo?" Tera asks.

"Nothing." I try my best to stay cool. Tera rolls her eyes.

"I already know you like Jake," Tera says in my ear. Jake is my friend, but I don't like him like a boyfriend. He goes to Safe Zone sometimes, so we've gotten to know each other pretty well, but that's it. Why does a swim party in the middle of April have to be so complicated? Why does *everything* have to be so complicated?

Later in the day, I learn that Tera gave everyone in our class except Megan an invitation. If Mrs. Washington knew that, she would call Tera's mom, but of course no one is going to say anything about it. I can't imagine how Megan must feel. Honestly, I don't even want to go to the party anymore, but if Tera and Riley stop being my friends I won't have anyone to sit with when Megan's not at school. Plus, it's horrible being made fun of every day when you're by yourself. Every time I look at Megan, she's smiling at me like she's trying to let me know she's still my friend.

"Jo, follow me," Tera says when we're playing Four

Corners. Mrs. Washington calls out corner number four and we're the first to get out. Megan and another girl in my class, Veronica, are the only ones still in the game. I should have stayed with Megan.

When Mom picks me up at school, she's wearing jeans and a green sweater. "How was the job fair?" I ask, tossing my backpack to the back seat.

"It was fine, how was school today?"

"Awesome! I got invited to a birthday party." Mom turns her head towards me as we stop at the intersection.

"Whose party is it?"

"One of my friends at school. It's a swim party, so can I please get a new bathing suit?" Mom is taking a sip of her water bottle and almost chokes.

"Swim party? Who has a swim party when it's fifty degrees outside? No you can't go to a swim party." I can feel my skin melting, I'm so mad. I *have* to go to Tera's party.

"Please, Mom, everybody's going. Plus Tera's my new best friend." Mom sighs.

"I thought Megan was your best friend." I stare out the window at the kids on the school bus passing by.

"Please, can I go? I promise I won't ask for anything else in my entire life. Please? Please?"

"Well, I do need to get everything packed up tomorrow," Mom says.

"We're moving tomorrow?"

"Not tomorrow, but we will be moving before the end of the month."

"But that's next week!"

"I told you we have to move, honey," Mom says. "But you don't have to change schools."

"Where are we moving?" I ask, afraid of the answer.

"Close by. We'll be staying with Ms. Karyn and Mr. Earl from church for a while." My entire body goes numb.

"But they have five boys and the little ones are all bad! None of them listen." I fold my arms across my chest.

"Joanna, why would you say that? Ms. Karyn and Mr. Earl are kind enough to allow us to stay with them in their home until I find another job. I don't ever wanna hear you talk like that again, do you understand?"

"Yes, ma'am." I don't know where I'm going to sleep. I can't share a room with a boy, no way. "What about all of our stuff?"

"I'm putting everything in storage and when we get another place we'll get everything out. Don't worry, everything's going to be fine." Mom keeps telling me not to worry and that "everything's going to be fine," but it's kind of hard when every day it seems like I have something new to worry about.

"So what kind of bathing suit do you want to pick out for the party?"

"I don't know," I mumble, trying not to let Mom see me cry.

"Listen, I understand this is a lot for you all at once, but I really need you to hang in there, okay? This is only temporary. While Mr. Earl and Ms. Karyn are helping me pack up our things, you'll be at the party. Isn't that much better?" I nod, but inside, I am screaming NO! I don't want to live with another family. I want to stay in our house with my own room and my own things. Mom puts her hand on my shoulder.

"It'll be okay, ladybug," she says as we drive into the mall parking lot.

Memory Verse 4

Matthew 6:26

'Look at the birds. They don't plant, harvest, or save food in barns, but your heavenly Father feeds them. Don't you know you are worth much more than they are?"

I can't eat anything. My stomach is making all kinds of weird noises. I hope it stops before the party. I place Emily on my bed next to my pillow then grab Tera's invitation from my backpack. I'm wearing my new swimsuit. Mom and I agreed on a plain purple one-piece with ruffles at the top; otherwise she wouldn't let me go to the swim party at all. Mom braids my hair into a side French braid.

"It's warmer than it's been all week," she says.

"Can I borrow your sunglasses?" Mom has tons of designer sunglasses.

"Sure, but not my new pair." I choose a pair of brown aviators because they match my hair.

"Where's your towel?" Mom hands me a water bottle.

"Tera says I don't need to bring one." I walk around the maze of empty brown boxes piled next to the front door.

On the way to Tera's house, I notice the houses are much bigger than where I live.

"What a beautiful neighborhood," Mom says, reading my mind. There are no abandoned grocery carts on the sidewalk or paper cups in the gutters. There's also a nice park with grass so green it doesn't even look real.

"I think this is it." Mom looks down at the invitation. Tera's house is the biggest on the entire block. It looks like a mansion. Alyssa and Ebony bolt out of the front door onto the gigantic front yard with handfuls of water balloons. I look down at my bathing suit; they're both wearing bikinis.

"I guess I'll say hello to Tera's mother."

"Can you just drop me off please? I'm ten years old," I remind her.

"Alright, open the glove compartment. There's a card inside for your friend. I bought her a twenty-five dollar gift card for the movie theater."

"Thanks!" I exclaim. I hope Tera likes it. She told me she likes going to the movies. Mom takes a slow deep breath and leans forward.

"Give me a kiss," she says, puckering her lips. Mom is wearing bright red lipstick so I kiss her cheek and wave goodbye.

"I'll be back at four," she says.

"Hey Joanna," Ebony says, smashing a red balloon against Alyssa's back. Dodging the balloons, I race into the house. Music vibrates in my body. At least ten kids, boys and girls, are dancing in the living room. Tera's house is humongous.

"Oh my gosh, Jo!" Tera shrieks. She's wearing make-up and a yellow bikini. Her hair is in a high bun. She pulls me into the circle of her jumping friends. I hand Tera the card.

"Thanks, why didn't you wear a bikini?" I make out her

words by reading her lips. Her voice is drowning in the music.

"My mom wouldn't buy me one," I holler with my hands cupped at the sides of my mouth.

"Wanna borrow mine?" she says, closer to my ear. She tosses the card on top of a mountain of gift bags and presents. My heart is hammering to the fast beats of Jeremy Joel's new song. In every direction, I see kids from school or kids I don't know, but I don't see any adults anywhere.

"C'mon!" Tera yanks me up the stairs.

"Where's Riley?" I ask, staring at all the pictures of Tera and her older sister on the walls. Tera looks like a model in every picture.

"Her parents are super strict and they wouldn't let her come." She frowns. I nod as we enter her bedroom. It smells like cotton candy and I feel like I'm on my favorite TV show where the kids have the most amazing rooms. The walls are painted to look like an ocean with sparkling glitter fish swimming around her bed. Her bed is a canopy with green and blue silky cloths draped around it. She has a big flat screen TV, cable, and every new game system with tons of games.

"Your closet is huge!" I walk inside. There are enough clothes and shoes for every girl in our class.

"This is nothing; you should see my sister's closet." Tera sits down on a black leather bench inside her closet.

"Try some on." She points to the bikinis she threw on her bed. I glance at her wide-open bedroom door. Anyone could walk in.

"Can I close the door?"

"Of course," Tera says, kicking the door closed. I take off my shorts and set them neatly on Tera's bed. The first bikini is blue with green little turtles on the top. I really like it.

"Blue is not your color—try the hot pink one," she says. I change into the hot pink one. It feels much tighter on the bottom.

"That's super cute Jo! Oh my gosh, you have to wear that one!" I smile a little. Someone is knocking on the door and I can hear my heart beating.

"What!" Tera screams.

"Your mom wants you to come down," the voice behind the door says. Tera rolls her eyes.

"In a minute!" She darts her eyes towards me and I reach for my shorts.

"Don't put your shorts on; you can't see the bikini with shorts on, silly." I follow Tera down the stairs. A woman I think is her mom because she looks exactly like Tera except older is in the kitchen pulling water bottles out of the package and setting them on the table.

"What are you doing, Tera? You have guests." She points toward the kitchen window, where I can see kids jumping in the pool.

"I'm letting my best friend Jo borrow my bikini," she says, wrapping her arm around me. I can't believe she called me her best friend!

"Hi," I wave.

"Hello, Jo. Get out there with your friends, Tera," her

21

mom orders. Tera and I walk with her arm still around me to the backyard pool.

"Oh my gosh, Jo—don't look, Jake is here," she says. I smile with my mouth closed and look at Jake, who is picking his nose.

"I have to change before my mom picks me up," I admit. Every minute in the bikini feels like an eternity. I don't think Tera heard me because she's putting on sunscreen she found on the patio table.

"Here, put some on." She hands me the bottle.

"Jo!" My heart stops. My mom is standing at the sliding glass door, holding the sunglasses I borrowed. I must have forgotten them in the car. She looks so mad.

"Let me talk to you for a minute," she says, veins bulging from her neck. I don't look at Tera or anyone else, I just follow Mom out of the front double doors. I can barely keep up with her, she's walking so fast.

"What are you wearing?" She squints her eyes at the bikini.

"Oh, Tera let me borrow her bathing suit." My voice is shaky. I can hear whispers behind me at the door.

"Why would you wear Tera's bathing suit when I just bought you a bathing suit? And didn't we talk about why I don't want you wearing a bikini?"

"Yes, ma'am."

"Get your things, let's go."

"But—" My lips are trembling.

"Joanna, I really don't want to have this conversation here and trust me, Lord Jesus, trust me, I don't think you want to either." I hold my breath and run past Tera up the stairs. I change in Tera's bathroom and hurry back downstairs without saying anything to anyone. Mom is waiting in the car. The entire ride home, Mom doesn't say anything. She just turns the radio up and stares at the road.

When we get home, there's a moving truck parked in front of our house. Mr. Earl and a man I don't recognize are carrying our couch to the truck.

"Get showered and changed, then come down for lunch," Mom says. I take my time in the shower, letting the steam fill the whole bathroom and fog the mirror. Tera probably hates me. I ruined her party.

Downstairs, I find a sandwich and chips sitting on a paper plate at the kitchen table. Ms. Karyn and Mom are talking, probably about me, outside on the patio. I can tell Mom is still mad because she's talking mostly with her hands and rubbing her head. Ms. Karyn puts her hand on Mom's shoulder and Mom shakes her head. I'm not hungry, but I take a bite of my sandwich anyway.

"Hey there, how was the party?" Mr. Earl asks, wiping his hands on his jeans.

"It was good." I take a sip of apple juice.

"Good," he says, lifting our coffee table. I wish I never would have put on the bikini; then none of this would have happened. Actually, I wish I never had gone to Tera's party. Ms. Karyn and Mom are walking into the house so I take another bite of my ham and cheese sandwich.

"Hi Joanna, how are you, sweetie?" Ms. Karyn asks.

"Hi, Ms. Karyn," I mumble, but Mom is giving me a

mean look so I add a smile. Ms. Karyn and Mom are wrapping up all of our dishes with newspapers and putting them into boxes.

"When you're finished eating, I want you to help, okay?" Mom says.

"Yes ma'am," I say, picking up my chip in slow motion. I take the smallest bite I can. By the time I'm finished, our living room looks like no one even lives here anymore. Tera's so lucky. She has everything and her mom is so cool for letting her wear bikinis and letting her have a swim party and a cell phone. I rest my hand against my cheeks. I wish I had Tera's life.

"Are you done eating?" Mom interrupts my thoughts. I stand next to Ms. Karyn and imagine I'm floating in Tera's pool. I bet everyone's having so much fun at Tera's party. I didn't even get to swim or eat cake and ice cream. Maybe if I had a cell phone I could call her and tell her how sorry I am for making a big scene at her party. I guess I'll have to wait until Monday—that is, if she still wants to be my friend.

Memory Verse 5

Jeremiah 29:11

"I say this because I know the plans that I have for you."
This message is from the Lord. "I have good plans for you. I
don't plan to hurt you. I plan to give you hope and a good
future."

When the moving truck drives away, there is nothing left
except the picture of Mom, Dad, and me when I was three, a
few lamps, and our blankets and pillows. Our clothes are
piled in black trash bags in the closet. Mom, Emily, and I are
sleeping on the floor next to the wall in Mom's room. I put
my pillows underneath my back.

"What's wrong?" Mom yawns.

"My back hurts." I wiggle, trying to get comfortable.

"I'm sorry," Mom sighs. I wish I hadn't said anything,
because she hands me her pillow.

"It's okay," I say, giving it back.

"Take it," she insists. I feel bad. Mom is resting her
head on her arms and I have three pillows. I can hear all
kinds of weird noises, but Mom says it's just the cracks in the
walls. Emily is so scared. I keep her close to me so she can't
see the shadows crawling up and down the walls. Mom
presses her hand against my head and rubs my scalp.

"Can't sleep?" she asks. I don't want to tell her that I
would be able to sleep if I had my bed. Or maybe if she read

me a story like she used to.

"Can you turn the light on?" I ask. Mom turns the light on, but it's much brighter than the light in my room.

"Better?" she asks. I nod and cover my head with the blankets. All I can think about are the bugs Mom told me were on the floor when I asked her why I couldn't eat in my room. I bet there are spiders too, and I hate spiders.

I can't remember when I fell asleep, but when I wake up it feels like I just went to sleep. We don't have our TV anymore, so Mom listens to the Saturday morning news on her phone instead.

"What's a recession?" I ask, while Mom twists my hair and curls the ends with her fingers.

"It's when there's a big drop in economic growth and a lot of people are without jobs so businesses sell fewer goods and services. Why do you ask?" Mom sounds like a human dictionary.

"It's pretty much all they talk about on the news," I say.

"You're right; it's affecting a lot of people right now."

"How long do you think it's going to take before you get another job?" Mom stops twisting my hair and looks at me in the bathroom mirror.

"Not long, but I told you I don't want you worrying about things." There's that word again, "worry." I'm surprised Mom hasn't brought up Tera's party, but then again she's pretty busy with everything we're trying not to worry about.

"What are we gonna do today?" Mom got us up at 7:00 this morning as if we were going to church.

"We're going to run some errands and pick up some things," she says, going back to twisting my hair. She hasn't twisted her hair in a while. It's pulled back into a bun. There are circles around her eyes that weren't there yesterday and she hasn't put her lipstick on.

"What?" She catches me staring at her.

"Nothing." I look down. When she's finished twisting my hair, she hands me a grocery bag filled with pennies, nickels, dimes, and quarters that I sit on my lap in the car. There's a trash bag filled with cans in the back seat. On the radio they're talking about unemployment and the recession again. It seems like that's all Mom wants to listen to.

"Can we listen to music?" I ask, but Mom is staring at the green light. The car behind us honks and Mom slams her hands on the steering wheel.

"What's your problem!" she screams, glaring into the rear view mirror. The car honks again and Mom honks back.

"People are so ridiculous! A whole two seconds at a stoplight and everyone's mad." The angry man behind us passes us by, but Mom doesn't notice his finger pointed at us. The first stop is the grocery store, where I pour all of the change into the coin machine. Mom gets a ticket and exchanges it for twenty dollars. We buy two cases of dry instant noodles, two bags of pinto beans, and lots of gallons of water. Next, we exchange the trash bags filled with cans for more money. I think Mom's forgotten about breakfast.

"Can we get something to eat?" I ask.

"Oh, I'm sorry honey, there's a banana in the glove compartment." I open the glove compartment and find a brown mushy banana. Mom is busy honking at another driver, so I decide to eat it even though it smells rotten.

"What is this place?" I ask. We drive into a parking lot filled with a long line of people.

"Grab my purse for me, will you?" Mom rushes out of the car. The line stretches all the way out of the building and wraps around it.

"Why are we standing in line?"

"Shh!" Mom waves at me. I take a deep breath. I'm still hungry and my mouth is sticky. The sun has moved away from the clouds and I'm starting to sweat underneath my gray sweater. It feels like we've been in line for an hour when we finally get to the front. A lady with long Nubian locks is standing at the door handing out boxes. She's wearing a T-shirt that says "Melanie's Food Pantry."

"I love your pretty hair," she says, lifting one of my twisted curls. Inside, the cool air feels good. It's a warehouse with green metal shelves with boxes and rows of canned food. Mom fills up the box with green beans, corn, peas, and boxes of brown rice. We stay for a few minutes before Mom says it's time to go. I help Mom fit the box into the trunk by moving the water to the side. The clock in the car says twelve and we haven't eaten lunch yet. Maybe we don't have money for lunch and Mom is hoping I don't ask. My stomach growls, but Mom doesn't hear it because she's listening to talk radio about the recession again.

"Are we going home now?" I ask. At least I can make a sandwich when we get home.

"Not yet. I still have a few more errands to run." I

don't know how much longer I can hide how hungry I am, because my stomach is growling louder and louder. I wrap my arms around my stomach and try not to think about it. We go to another building for more canned vegetables, standing in line for another hour. At least they give us water bottles. Mom hasn't eaten anything, not even a rotten banana, and she gave me her water bottle. I can see sweat on her forehead so I know she's thirsty even though she says she's not every time I offer her a drink of mine.

It's three o'clock and we're finally back home. Mom makes me a package of noodles, but I'm still hungry after I finish eating. The refrigerator is empty except for water, ketchup, mustard, grape jelly, and a carton of milk that expired yesterday. All of the sandwich meat is gone.

"Wanna go to the library?" Mom asks, rubbing her eyes. I say yes, because I can tell she's bored too. When we get there, the library is crowded and there's no place to sit. I pick out a book about a boy who becomes invisible and Mom picks out a dozen books on resumes and job interviews.

"What's wrong, ladybug?" Mom asks when we get back home.

"Nothing," I sit on the floor and open my book.

"You've hardly said anything all day." She sits down beside me. I keep reading my book, hoping she'll stop tempting me to tell her I'm still hungry.

"Can we go swimming at the community pool tomorrow?" I ask, thinking about Tera's pool.

"Swimming? It's still not hot enough." She sucks in air, looks up toward the ceiling, then down at me. "I'm sorry we left the party."

Why is Mom apologizing to me? I'm the one who should be apologizing.

"I shouldn't have borrowed Tera's bathing suit," I mumble.

"Well, no you shouldn't have—but we could have talked about it when you got home. I noticed the other girls had bikinis on so I can understand why you changed. I'm not saying it was right, but I understand."

"Everybody did," I confess.

"I know," she says pulling me closer to her. "When I was your age, your grandmother didn't let me wear bikinis either. I had to swim in my regular clothes."

"Regular clothes? Like jeans?" How embarrassing.

"Not jeans, shorts and a t-shirt. We didn't have a lot of money for extra things like bathing suits—and there's no way she would *ever* let me run around wearing a bikini, especially in the small town I grew up in." Mom laughs. "I guess I've picked up a lot of her ways."

"Grandma Jean was always so nice to me." I try to picture her telling Mom to wear regular clothes to the pool.

"She was much older and very sick then," Mom says.

"A lot of kids wear bikinis now." I wait for Mom to say, *"You're not a lot of kids."* But she doesn't. She just rubs my back and listens to me explain all the things kids are allowed to have and do now, like a cell phone, and sleepovers, and sports, and fun things like gymnastics or dance. Most kids don't have to sleep on the floor like me, or stand in long lines for food—at least not most of the kids I know.

Memory Verse 6

Psalms 34:18
"The Lord is close to those who have suffered
disappointment.
He saves those who are discouraged."

"Everybody freeze!" Ms. Bethany calls out from the stage. We're dancing and jumping to the song "Undignified" and freezing when the music stops. I'm standing on one shaky leg and my arms are making a "V" in the air. Kiara has bubbles in her cheeks—she's trying hard not to laugh. We bump into each other and fall to the floor when the song is over.

"Your head feels like a bowling ball," Kiara laughs, rubbing her head. It's time to get into our small groups. Kiara pulls a white envelope from her purple Bible that has her name engraved into it.

"This weekend's my birthday party!" I take the invitation and stuff it into my dad's dusty black and brown Bible Mom let me borrow since mine is in a box somewhere.

"Aren't you gonna look at it?" Kiara frowns. She's wearing new zebra-print glasses and colorful sandals I've never seen before. They show off her painted sparkling purple toenails that match her fingernails. Her mom flat-ironed her hair, and she flips it behind her every other second. Her jeans have pink stars on them that match her silky pink shirt. I open the invitation and it's a picture of Kiara wearing a white princess dress and a diamond crown. She's sitting in a red velvet and gold chair like she's the queen. "JOIN THE PRINCESS AND CELEBRATE HER 10TH BIRTHDAY!" the invitation says. I roll my eyes and stuff it back into the envelope. Good for her.

"I can't go," I say as Ms. Bethany asks us to join our group. Kiara raises the corner of her top lip and makes a smacking sound with her teeth.

"You're acting stank today," she says, getting in line behind me. I can't ask my mom for more money for another gift and since Kiara's my best friend at church I want to get her something nice, something expensive like a gold bracelet or a heart locket.

"My mom won't let me," I say.

"How do you know when you didn't even ask her?" Kiara blows her hot breath in my face.

"I just know," I say without turning around.

"Mmmhmm…I'm gonna ask her when she picks you up."

"You can't!" Ms. Bethany and all the other girls in our line glare at me.

"Somebody woke up on the wrong side of the bed," Kiara whispers. I bite my nails until we sit in a circle on the green carpet inside of the classroom. I can see Kiara staring at me in the corner of my eye, but I keep my eyes on Ms. Bethany. Today's lesson is about forgiveness.

"How was your week, girls?" Ms. Bethany pulls her blonde hair into a ponytail.

"Can I go first?" Leah asks. Every week she wants to go first. If we play a game she has to be the leader; if it's time to pray she wants to pray. Ms. Bethany smiles, but I can tell she's thinking the same thing I'm thinking: *Let somebody else go first for a change!*

"Sure, Leah," Ms. Bethany says instead.

"I went to the movies and then I went ice skating," she says, puffing out her chest.

"Awesome," Ms. Bethany says.

"I'm good at ice skating, so I rarely fall," Leah brags, even though nobody asked her. Kiara is next and then it's my turn. I need to think of something to say and fast. I could say I went to the library, but that sounds so boring. Or I went to a birthday party, a swim party.

"Me and my brother went to feed the homeless. We also donated canned foods and clothes to the poor people," Kiara says. My face feels like it's stuck in a wood-fired pizza oven. I'm "the poor people" she's talking about. That's why I wear the same blue and white sneakers with dirty shoelaces every week, and why I haven't gotten any new outfits in so long I can't even remember. What if she saw me at the food pantry? What if the canned goods are the ones she gave?

"That's so great, Kiara. There are so many poor people who need food and clothes. What a nice thing for you and your brother to do," Ms. Bethany says. I wish I could rip up Kiara's invitation right in front of her. I can feel tears ready to pop out of my eyes.

"What about you, Joanna, what did you do this week?" I blink and a tear spills out. I get up.

"I need to use the bathroom," I say, but my voice sounds like it's crying.

"Oh, okay," Ms. Bethany says. The bathroom is down the hallway. It's empty. I close the door and let the rest of the tears free. They rush down my face like a waterfall. Some of them I catch in my mouth. They taste like beach water, which reminds me of why we can't go back to the beach. I wish I had Emily to tell me being poor isn't embarrassing. But it *is* embarrassing, because everyone knows. They can tell by my clothes, my shoes, Mom's old noisy rusted car, my holey backpack, and especially if they come to our house. We have nothing. No videogames, no cable, no food in the refrigerator…. The waterfall won't stop and it's flooding my mouth, along with a little bit of snot.

"Joanna? Are you in here?" Kiara calls. Why is she here? She opens the door and sees the waterfall and snot and me standing in front of the toilet.

"What's wrong," she says, pulling me out with both arms. I can't tell her, *"I'm the poor person you helped."* Or *"I can't go to your party because I don't have any money to buy you a stupid present."*

"Joanna? What's wrong?" she asks again. I don't answer. I can't. I'm too mad. I know it's not her fault she has a lot of stuff and her parents have nice jobs and make a lot of money, but I don't want to be friends with her anymore.

"I'm fine." My voice sounds like a cough melted into my words.

"No you're not, tell me why you're crying." She pushes me. I push back, making my way towards the door. Ms.

Bethany comes in. Great.

"What's going on?" she asks, like I'm a fragile baby.

"I don't know," Kiara says, trying to prove her innocence. Ms. Bethany tells Kiara to go back and gives me a hug. Now church is ruined. Everybody's gonna ask Kiara, "What's wrong with Joanna?" and "Why is Joanna crying?" They're going to tell their parents, "This girl in church was crying." The whole church is going to stare at me and know it's because I'm poor.

"Joanna, you don't have to tell me what's wrong, only if you want to, okay? Whatever it is just know that God loves you and I love you too," she says. I'm glad I don't have to tell her. It's none of her business and she's only acting like she doesn't know. Just like everyone else.

"Do you want to go back?"

"In a minute," I say.

"Okay, do you need someone to get your mom?" I shake my head hard and fast. *Please, please don't tell my mom!*

"No, I'm okay," I say in a cheerful voice. I even fake a smile.

"Is everything okaaaay?" Ms. Bethany's voice is begging me to tell her.

"I just—" I want to tell her, but I can't. She'll talk to Mom, and Mom will be so embarrassed and we'll never go back to church again. Why did I have to start crying?

"Is everything OK at home?" Ms. Bethany asks. Ugh! Now she thinks Mom is feeding me to a poor people-eating monster that lives under the stairs. I wanna say, "Everything is fine at home, I'm just poor!" Maybe I can just tell her a little bit so that she'll stop looking at me like I'm a cute puppy stuck in a tree.

"I'm really sad that I can't go to Kiara's birthday party. I went to a swim party over the weekend and I got in trouble and now I can't go," I say, checking her eyes to see if they believe me. Her eyebrows straighten and she takes a deep breath.

"Well, it's normal to feel that way. Sometimes we make bad choices, but the good thing is we can make better choices the next time right?"

I nod. "Mmm-hmmm."

"I'll give you a minute to get cleaned up, okay?" She's talking about my gross snot-nose. She leaves and I feel better. Mom will never know what happened, but I have to be more careful. I can't cry like that anymore. I pinch myself until I want to cry. I can fight the waterfall if I build an invisible Hoover Dam. *This can never happen again, Joanna*, I scold myself.

When I get back to the group, just like I predicted, everyone is staring at my red eyes. I think of the Hoover Dam. I've seen it three times and it's so strong; it's as thick as two football fields and 726 feet tall. If I want to have more power, I have to build a Hoover Dam around me so I can control the floods.

Memory Verse 7

1 John 4:19
"We love because God first loved us."

It's Monday, and I begged Mom to let me wear black shorts so I can match Tera and Riley, but Tera didn't come to school and Riley hasn't said a word to me all morning. I bet Tera told her I ruined her party, because Riley's not wearing her black shorts. Megan is wearing the same pants and shirt she wore on Friday. I'm glad Tera's not here to make fun of her.

"We will all be getting to know a very special person," Mrs. Washington says. We look around the room. She stops at my desk.

"Joanna, will you please stand up?"

"Me?" Everyone is staring at me.

"For the month of May, Joanna is going to be our star student of the month." Everyone cheers and claps for me. It's nothing special—we clap for every star student—but it does feel kind of nice. Mrs. Washington gives me a poster board, a paper for Mom to fill out about me, and a notebook to write anything I want to share with the class for my star student presentation. I have no idea what I'm going to talk about, but at least I have a few weeks to figure it out. I look around the room at all of the star student poster boards.

Tera's poster has pictures of her gymnastics competitions. During Tera's presentation we watched a DVD of her on the balance beam and she talked about her dreams of becoming an Olympic gymnast. She even did a few backflips outside. Megan hasn't been a star student yet. I wonder what she'll talk about when she is. She never talks about gymnastics, dance class, or soccer like the other girls in my class. Now that I think about it, she hardly talks about her life outside of school at all.

It's lunchtime, so I stuff my notebook inside my desk, crushing old homework papers and an alligator sock puppet I made in art. Riley is whispering to this kid named Evan. I think she likes him, because her mouth is frozen like a Popsicle—a smile Popsicle. We're having hot dogs for lunch, and they look disgusting. Most of them are burnt, and the ones that aren't have little beads of sweat on them. Holding my tray of sweaty hot dog, tater tots, applesauce, and chocolate milk, I look around the cafeteria. Riley is sitting with Evan and Jake. Megan is sitting at the end of the long white table by herself.

"Hey," I say, hoping she won't scream "TRAITOR!" Megan smiles at me, so I sit down, thankful she still wants to be friends. We're both staring at our hot dogs. I'm hungry but not sweaty hot dog hungry.

"Looks gross, huh?" I say, opening my chocolate milk. Megan has already taken a bite.

"It's not that bad," she says. I can see smashed hot dog bun pieces on both sides of her mouth. My hotdog feels slimy and cold when I drop it into the stiff white chalky bun.

I take a bite and she's right, it could be worse. It could be liver and onions. Mom loves liver and onions. They always make me want to throw up because they smell like someone already did.

"How was your weekend?" Megan asks. Does she know I went to Tera's party?

"It was okay, how was yours?"

Megan shrugs. "Someone stole my bag so now I don't have anything to wear."

"Your bag?" I take another bite.

"Yeah, all of my clothes were in a bag at the Laundromat and when we went to buy more laundry soap, someone stole it."

"What's a Laundromat?" I ask. Megan looks confused, like she just solved a two-thousand piece puzzle and there's one puzzle piece missing.

"You don't know what a Laundromat is?"

"No." I can see the teddy bear hamster in my head running fast on my brain wheel. The hamster stops running and says, "*Uh-oh, I've got nothing on a Laundromat—is that bad?*"

"It's where people wash their clothes."

"I wash my clothes at home," I say. Megan's eyes relax and she nods.

"Oh…"

"So you don't have *any* clothes left?" My brain wheel hurts just thinking about that.

"Nope, just the clothes I'm wearing. They stole everything, even my underwear."

"What are you going to do? You can't keep wearing the

same clothes every day."

"I don't know," Megan says. We sit in silence. Who would steal someone's underwear? I picture a thief wearing a black mask and black and white striped pajamas creeping into the Laundromat. *"Where do they hide the underwear?"* he says in a dark and creepy voice. I shiver. That's a weird thought. I can't believe someone stole Megan's clothes and she has nothing to wear. Maybe her mom lost her job too and she doesn't have any money to buy her more clothes. If I were Megan and I only had one outfit to wear I would never go back to school. I would hide in the itchy bushes with bugs and whatever else hides in bushes all day long, just so Tera and Riley wouldn't make fun of me. Actually, I think the whole school would make fun of me if I wore the same clothes every day. Megan is so calm, maybe she doesn't care if people make fun of her, but I care: she can't wear the same clothes every day.

"I have tons of clothes—maybe you could borrow some until you get some new clothes," I whisper. I don't want Megan to feel bad about not having any clothes and I don't want the whole table to hear. Mom says nosy people can smell gossip like a juicy steak. Looking at the kids at our table, they would much rather eat a juicy gossip steak instead of sweaty hot dogs any day.

"Really?" Megan's face lights up like a Christmas tree.

"Yeah." I nod like it's no big deal, but I probably should have asked Mom first before I opened my big mouth. I can hear Mom saying, *"Joanna, put that gossip steak down! Maybe her Mom doesn't want you in their business? You should have*

40

asked me before you volunteered to give away your clothes. Clothes don't grow on trees you know." Megan's smile fades, she leans over and her back sticks out like the Hunchback of Notre Dame.

"But how are you going to get them to me before tomorrow?" I hadn't thought about that. After school I usually run as fast as I can to the playground and Megan's already gone.

"You can come to my house," I say. I don't care that my house is empty—this is an emergency. There's no way Megan can wear the same outfit tomorrow. That would be worse than eating Brussels sprouts every day for a whole year!

"I have to ask my mom," Megan says.

"Me too."

"I don't have a cell phone to call her."

"Me either." Riley has a phone. She's texting on it right now.

"I can ask Riley if I can borrow her phone," I suggest. We both look at Riley. Riley gives us the same look I give Mom when the dentist says I have a cavity.

"Can you wait for me to ask my mom after school?" Megan asks. That *would* give me time to explain things to Mom, because she hates when I say I'm going to do something without talking to her first. She always says, *"Did you ask me?"* and I always say, *"Oops…sorry…"* and then she says, *"You better ask me first."* But this is an emergency. Megan only has one pair of underwear!

"Yeah, I can do that," I say. Megan sits up and finishes her chocolate milk. I put my applesauce in my pocket. The bell rings and we line up together. If Tera would have been at school I never would have known that someone had stolen Megan's clothes, because I would have sat with Tera. I look behind me at Megan. She's always been nice to me even when I ignored her. I've been a horrible friend, but at least she's giving me another chance. Mom might be mad, but I have to help Megan no matter what. I pull my applesauce out of my pocket and sneak it to Megan.

"Thanks," she says, putting it in her other pocket.

"No problem," I answer. All I can think about is how I'm going to explain things to Mom.

Memory Verse 8

Genesis 16:13
"Don't worry—I am with you.
Don't be afraid—I am your God.
I will make you strong and help you.
I will support you with my right hand that brings victory."

I have no more nails left to bite by the time Megan and I walk out to the blacktop with our class. The bell rings, and it looks like Disneyland minus the rides and the churros. I don't see Mom. Kids are pushing into me, forcing my backpack sideways, and parents are blocking my view. Megan follows my trail like a mouse through a people maze.

"My mom's over there." She points to the yellow slide and gives Mrs. Washington a high-five to let her know she sees her parent.

I don't see Mom anywhere. Megan trips over her shoelaces on the way to her mom. I look towards Safe Zone, where kids are walking into the cafeteria; sometimes Mom waits for me there by the water fountain. Mrs. Washington is looking at her watch and back at me. There's only me and three other kids in our class still waiting.

"Do you see your parent, Joanna?" Mrs. Washington asks. She told us this morning she had to pick up her daughter from the airport after school and she didn't want to be late. At the playground (no Mom), on the blacktop (no

Mom), some parents are waiting in the shade leaning against the school wall (still no Mom). Where is she?

Mr. Suarez, our principal, is standing at the gate with a walkie-talkie. They're going to close the gate soon. The other kids are gone now, and I'm the only one waiting with Mrs. Washington. Megan and her mom are waiting for me. Megan waves for me to come.

"Can I go talk to Megan really quick?" I ask Mrs. Washington.

"No, you need to stay right here and wait for your parent. Who's coming to pick you up?"

"My mom," I sigh. Megan's mom grabs her hand and now they're leaving. Megan's looking back at me because I let her down.

"Let's go," Mrs. Washington snaps. She's walking so fast I can't keep up. We walk through the cafeteria into the office. Mrs. Washington tells the front office lady my name and says my mom isn't here in a deep voice like the evil Dr. Boom in a cartoon I watch sometimes.

"Have a seat," the front office lady with red hair says. Mrs. Washington jogs out of the office without saying goodbye. I look at the clock hanging above the office lady with blonde hair. The bell rang at 3:20. It's now 3:50 and Mom's *still* not here. The red-haired office lady tells Mr. Suarez that my mom didn't come to pick me up and she's not answering the phone.

"What do you want me to do?" she asks Mr. Suarez. The office closes at four. Mr. Suarez taps the long black walkie-talkie antennae on his wrinkled forehead. Just then,

Mom walks in.

"I'm so sorry!" she says, out of breath. "I had an emergency. I got here as soon as I could." An emergency? I had an emergency too!

"Let's go, ladybug," she says, like everything's fine. When we get outside, most of the kids are gone and the crossing guard is walking towards her car parked in front of the school.

"Where were you?" I slap my hands against my legs.

"The car wouldn't start," Mom says, walking fast.

"Where are we going?"

"We have to walk to Ms. Karyn's house," she says.

"But you said we weren't moving yet."

"Joanna! I got here as fast as I could, okay? I don't need to listen to you whine right now. I'm sorry I was late, but the car wouldn't start and I got here as fast as I could." Ms. Karyn's house is really far and I don't feel like walking. We pass the grocery store and the gas station.

"Can we get some water?" I ask.

"We're almost there," Mom says. What that means is, "no," not because she doesn't want to, but because she doesn't have the money to.

"But they have a drinking fountain inside. It doesn't cost anything. You won't have to spend any money." Mom stops walking and glares down at me.

"Is that what you think? That I don't have the money?" I don't say anything. The Hoover Dam around me is keeping me safe. Mom looks different. Her face is skinny, and the circles around her eyes are bigger and darker. She laughs like when someone is being sarcastic.

"C'mon!" She yanks on my arm and we walk into the grocery store parking lot. Mom buys me a water bottle and we don't talk to each other the rest of the way to Ms. Karyn's house.

Ms. Karyn's house is brown and white. It has two stories and there's a red van parked in the driveway next to Mom's car. Why couldn't Ms. Karyn give Mom a ride to pick me up from school? I don't want to ask. Not now.

Inside, it smells like food and my stomach growls. Ms. Karyn and Mr. Earl have a lot of nice furniture and pictures. They have a huge flat screen TV, bigger than the one in Tera's room, and a cable box. I hear laughter and rumbling coming from upstairs; the wild boys are up there. I imagine that Ms. Karyn's house is a South African safari: Mom is a lion, Ms. Karyn is the giraffe because she's tall, and the boys are the spotted hyenas. Mr. Earl is the hippopotamus, because he is so quiet he could be sleeping, and hippos that fall asleep under water can rise out of the water and breathe without waking up. I'm a famous explorer with a South African accent, wearing a green camouflage hat, a brown cargo vest, and brown shorts. My binoculars are the O's I make with my hands in front of my eyes. *"Watch out for the lion,"* my assistant warns, and I say, *"Rr-eye-ight mate,"* in my accent, but I let it roll together so you can just hear the "eye" in right.

"Hello, Ms. Joanna, would you like to wash your hands and help me set the table for dinner?" Ms. Karyn asks. Mom gives me a stern look.

"Yes ma'am," I say. The bathroom has a fancy silky lace towel hanging beside the sink so I dry my hands on my pants. Ms. Karyn has made homemade potato salad, green beans, baked chicken, and rolls. It's so delicious. The boys gobble up their food at the wooden round table like Tasmanian devils. Ben, their older brother I've never met before, only eats his chicken, Ben has a mustache, and he's wearing a jacket with the name of his high school on it. The hyena boys are homeschooled—that's why they don't go to my school. One of the hyenas, Malachi, who is a year younger than me, keeps kicking my ankle underneath the table. Mom is finally smiling again so I pretend I don't notice and move my foot.

"Joanna, how was school today?" Ms. Karyn asks.

"It was good," I say. Malachi is sinking in his chair trying to find my foot so I wrap it around Mom's foot. I give him a look that says, *"Try kicking me now."* I think he gets the message, because he squints his eyes until I can barely see his pupils and pokes out his lips. My stomach is so full I accidently burp. The hyenas laugh and D'mari (he's seven) hangs out of his chair, swinging his neck back and forth while holding his stomach.

"That's enough," Mr. Earl growls.

"What do you say?" Mom says.

"Excuse me," I say. The hyenas keep laughing with puffy cheeks until Mr. Earl stares them all down. I need Emily. After I help Mom wash the dishes and do my homework, we go upstairs to our room to get ready for bed. We have our own TV with cable and a closet, but our clothes are in a pile against the wall next to our shoes. Even though I have to share a room with Mom, it's a pretty room with a thick white comforter and six pillows. We also have our own bathroom that the hyenas can't use.

"Where's Emily?" I ask Mom as I'm putting my pajamas on. Mom's eyes grow wide and she gasps.

"Oh no!" she groans, hitting her forehead with her hand. "I am soooo sorry—I must have forgotten her at the house."

"Let's go get her." I start looking for my shoes.

"We can't, honey, I've already given the landlord the keys. I'm so sorry. I'll buy you another doll." I can't breathe. Emily is alone in the dark and she's afraid of the dark.

"Can you talk to the landlord?" Mom shakes her head.

"I'll get you another doll, honey, I just—I'm sorry."

"Please?" The Hoover Dam is breaking.

"Alright, I'll see what I can do." Mom saves the Dam just in time. I crawl into bed with mom. Mom reads me two chapters of the story about the invisible boy, then closes the book and places it on her lap.

"I'm sorry I snapped at you today," she says.

"It's okay." I trace the letters on the book with my fingers.

"What did you do at school today?" she asks.

"Just school stuff," I say.

"Like what?"

"I went to specials and—" I remember that the star student paper is in my backpack for Mom, but she's yawning and it's late.

"What are specials?" she asks, even though I've told her like a gazillion times.

"Music and art." I yawn too. Yawns are contagious.

"How's your friend Tera?" Mom asks. I shake my head.

"She wasn't at school today."

"What about your other friend? Megan? How's Megan?"

"Fine," I mumble.

"I want you to know you can always talk to me, okay? I like to hear about your day and your friends," Mom says, playing with my hair.

"Okay." I close my eyes.

"Hey—" Mom shakes me. "Don't forget to say your prayers."

I say my prayers and ask God to help Megan. Mom is snoring. I can't sleep, but at least Mom's left the light on for me. I look over at the bags full of our clothes. I have an idea.

Memory Verse 4

Proverbs 30:5
"You can trust this: Every word that God speaks is true.
God is a safe place for those who go to him."

My holey purple backpack is bulging with clothes. Two pairs
of jeans, two pairs of shorts, two shirts, four pairs of socks,
and four pairs of underwear that I've barely worn; Megan
already has one outfit to wear so that will make five outfits.
My backpack is toppled over next to the table.

Ms. Karyn made all of us the biggest breakfast I've ever
seen. She made blueberry pancakes with real blueberries, a
yogurt parfait with strawberries, blackberries, raspberries,
and granola, and turkey bacon because it's healthier. The
hyena boys are so lucky to have so much food all the time.
They're really quiet at the table because Mr. Earl is reading
the newspaper. The living room has turned into "specials."
The hyenas play instruments like the guitar, the violin, the
cello, and the saxophone, and there are art supplies scattered
across the floor. I wish I could stay home with them because
it looks so fun. Ms. Karyn is so nice; she never yells at the
hyenas. I've already eaten two pancakes and a bowl full of
yogurt parfait, and my stomach is as stuffed as my backpack.
Mom drinks the last of her orange juice and thanks Ms.
Karyn.

"We gotta go," she says, looking down at her watch. It's only 7:30, but Mom has a job interview so I'm going to Safe Zone. I saw Ms. Karyn give Mom some money last night, and even though Mom tried to give it back, she kept it. Mom doesn't say anything about my backpack even though it looks like I crammed two big pillows inside of it. Maybe I'm turning invisible like the invisible boy. If I were really invisible I'd become a superhero that saves animals. And then I would talk for animals and people would know animals could talk. Maybe I could make a dog become really famous for telling jokes and he would have his own comedy show called "The Ruff Life."

"Joanna!" Mom's icy voice freezes my body. "Are you listening to me?"

"Yes ma'am," I say.

"Then what did I say?" Uh-oh, no clue. Maybe she said, *"Joanna I think being an invisible superhero that talks for animals is an ah-maze-zing idea, but you should really think about talking for cats; they are way more funny. But one question, what would your costume look like?"*

"Sorry," I say, because I don't think she can read my mind...or can she?

"Go grab a sweater. It's a little chilly this morning." Actually I think I'll grab a spoon and maybe some cheddar cheese? I love cheese in my chili. I have too many sweaters to choose from. That's what I forgot! What if Megan gets cold? I don't think she has a sweater. I wear two sweaters—a thin white sweater for Megan and a zip-up sweater that is two sizes too big for me but Mom bought it anyway because she says I'll "grow into it." When I zip up the sweater I look really weird, but Mom doesn't notice. She talks on her cell phone the entire walk to school about how much money she's going to get from "unemployment." She doesn't notice that I look like a land-based crustacean known as a roly-poly bug, although some people call them potato bugs. At Safe Zone, Mom waves bye with her left hand and holds her cell phone with her right hand.

"What do you have in that backpack?" Ms. Sims, the Safe Zone teacher, asks as I throw it on top of the pile of backpacks.

"Just stuff," I say. I guess I'm not invisible.

"School stuff, I hope." Ms. Sims looks over her red glasses. I smile and she moves on to the circle of giggling girls. Ms. Sims says, "Either everybody plays or nobody plays," because she doesn't like to see kids not being invited to play. Megan is walking on the blacktop. My heart jumps like a carpet mite. She's wearing a long red shirt that looks like it might be her mom's and the same pants she wore yesterday. Ms. Sims is talking to a parent about something, so I creep out the door; the cafeteria is so noisy no one hears the door creaking.

"Megan!" Running faster than The Flash, I grab her hand. "C'mon!"

"Where are we going? The bell's going to ring."

"I know, hurry!" I pull Megan into the cafeteria and dash to my backpack. We sprint into the gross bathroom and I open my backpack.

"Look," I say. My chest is rising and falling. I hand

Megan the clothes, but the socks fall to the floor.

"Eww, pick them up!" Megan changes into a pair of green shorts and a pink and green shirt.

"My mom bought me underwear," Megan says, looking at my underwear like they have moldy cheese on them. I almost forgot about the sweater. Megan loooooves the sweater. I got it for Easter last year and the buttons look like pearls.

"It gets so cold at night," Megan says, looking at the sweater in the dirty mirror. She gives me a hug and the socks fall on the nasty floor again.

"Meg-gan!"

"Sorry," she says, I help her put everything into her backpack because she has no idea what gross things I've seen on the floor. (Yeah—those things).

"Thank you so much!" Megan's eyes look like someone told her she doesn't have to stay at school today because she's going to the beach. By the time the bell rings, Megan looks fantastic. We line up together and everything is perfect…until I hear Tera calling me.

"Jo! Come up here!" I pretend like I don't hear her, but her voice gets louder. "Jo!"

"I think Tera wants you to go up there," Megan says. Now I'm pretending like I didn't hear Megan. Mrs. Washington saves the day by telling Tera to settle down. Keeping my head down, I walk into the classroom. Why did Mrs. Washington have to move me next to Tera?

"Did you miss me yesterday?" Tera asks. I don't say anything. Mrs. Washington answers a call from her cell phone. I can tell it's something personal because she's talking low into the phone.

"I didn't come to school because my mom had the day off so she wanted to take me to lunch and then we went to The Strip to see the new hotels. She bought me a new bracelet, see?" She shoves a sparkling bracelet in my face.

"That's cool," I say.

"Yeah she said she's going to pick a day every month just for me and her, even if it's a school day." I smile and nod my head.

"Look what Riley texted me." Tera hands me her phone.

Riley: Oh my gosh Joanna is being such a little brat today, I wish you were here. ☹

Tera: Why????

Riley: She's sitting with Megan! Why are you even friends with her???

I don't know what to say, but I feel like I'm going to throw up. The room is spinning. "Why didn't you sit with Riley? She's so mad," Tera whispers. I shrug my shoulders. "Riley hates you now," Tera says. I glance at Riley, who gives me a look like she just ate super-sour candy and hot sauce.

"I don't care," I say. Tera's eyes get big and she laughs. Then I realize she's laughing at Megan.

"Megan looks so dirty," she says, loud enough I know Megan can hear because Lilia is sitting next to Megan and now she's staring at Megan. My stomach feels light and I can't breathe. Tera is texting Riley that Megan stinks and Riley laughs too. It's like I'm the next performer on a big stage and thousands of people are watching me. The spotlight follows me as I walk onto the stage. I take the microphone. The crowd gets quiet. All I can see is Megan.

"Don't talk about my friend like that," I say. Tera is staring at me. I can't believe I said it out loud. I said it *so* loud everyone is staring at me, including Mrs. Washington.

"Joanna, come here please," Mrs. Washington says. I'm going to be in so much trouble.

"What's going on?"

"Tera keeps making fun of Megan and I'm sick of it." My heart is beating, "I-can't-believe-you-said-that!" like "boom-boom-boom-boom-boom-boom-boom! Mrs. Washington tilts her head to one side and her eyebrows do a dance.

"What do you mean, Tera is making fun of Megan?"

"Shecallsherdirtyallthetime!" the words pour out of my mouth. The class is so quiet I can hear the fly on Mrs. Washington's desk rubbing its legs together.

"Thank you for telling me. That was very brave," Mrs. Washington says. I don't feel brave. I feel like I'm diving into a pool and I'm not sure if there's water at the bottom. I can hear Tera's heart beating as I'm dropping to the bottom.

"I want you to go to the office so we can discuss this privately." The office? I've never been sent to the office before. I'm walking towards the door and I look at Tera. She looks like she's gonna cry, but when I look at Megan I feel better, because Megan doesn't deserve to be treated like this. Nobody does.

Memory Verse 10

Ephesians 4:32
"Be kind and loving to each other. Forgive each other the same as God forgave you through Christ."

Mr. Suarez straightens his red and white striped tie.

"Joanna? Can you tell me what's going on?" His phone is ringing. Saved by the phone. He looks at the phone, back at me, back to the phone, back at me, back to the phone, and now back at me. Answer the phone! I need more time to think!

"Um, well…" What if he calls my mom? Does he have to call my mom? Mr. Suarez is still waiting for me to say something. It's kind of like I'm on a game show and I have to pick door number one or door number two. The game show host says in a low deep voice, *"Which door is Joanna going to choose? Will she choose door number one and tell Mr. Suarez everything? Or will she choose door number two and say nothing?"* Both doors are gold with diamonds on the door handle, but I can only choose one.

"Joanna?" Mr. Suarez raises his eyebrows. I can hear the drumroll. I look at Mr. Suarez and point to door number one.

"I pick door number one!" I think with my eyes closed. *"Ladies and gentlemen, Joanna Miller has chosen door number one. Let's see what's behind door number one."*

"Tera has been making fun of Megan for a long time. She calls her "dirty" and she's really mean to her. She used to be mean to me, but then she stopped. I just want her to stop making fun of Megan," I say.

"Have you talked to Mrs. Washington?" Mr. Suarez asks.

"No, well, just today."

Mr. Suarez nods. "Thank you for bringing this to my attention; you know it's important that you let someone know as soon as you see another student being unkind."

"I know," I say. Mr. Suarez picks up the phone and tells the office lady to "Send Tera down." The game show host's "lovely assistant" opens door number one.

"It's Tera!" the audience gasps. Mr. Suarez and I don't say anything to each other. I peel my fingernails until the door opens and Tera walks in. She sits right next to me.

"Tera, Joanna says you've been calling Megan names." Tera's crying. I sink in my chair. Tera confesses to everything and Mr. Suarez explains bullying is "never tolerated."

"I'm so, so sorry," Tera sniffs.

"It's okay," I say. Mr. Suarez tells me I can go back to class, but I leave the door cracked.

"I'm going to have to have a conference with your parents," Mr. Suarez says.

"My mom and dad don't live with each other anymore. They're getting a divorce," Tera says as Mr. Suarez pushes the door closed.

Mrs. Washington tells me I won't be sitting behind Tera anymore. Now I'm sitting by Jake and Evan. Megan got sent to the principal's office too. So the whole day feels like I'm stuck inside a tornado with Tera, Riley, and Megan swirling around me. The wind is pushing me around so fast. Mom is in the tornado too and she's yelling, *"Why didn't you tell me!"*

"Joanna?"

"Yes?"

"Would you like to read?" I stare down at the hardcover book in front of me. I don't know what page we're on.

"Right here," Jake whispers, pointing to the second paragraph on page 65. I read until Mrs. Washington tells me to stop. Then Megan comes back. I wonder when Tera is coming back. Mrs. Washington answers the brown phone hanging on the wall. She mumbles something into the phone.

"Okay everyone, settle down. I want you reading silently for the next twenty minutes," she says, setting the timer on her desk. Riley is glaring at me like she has burning red lasers in her eyes. I look away, but I can still feel her lasers burning holes through me. When the bell rings, Tera is back. She seems normal. She's looking at her cell phone on the way to the blacktop.

Mom is waiting for me on the blacktop wearing work clothes. So is Megan's mom. Megan runs to her mom and shows her the clothes. They're walking over to us.

"Joanna, wait!" Megan races towards me. What is she doing? Mom turns around.

"Hi, I'm Stacy, Megan's mom," she says. Megan is grinning like she's not ruining everything.

58

Mom shakes Megan's mom's hand.

"Camille," Mom says.

"I just wanted to thank you so much for the clothes, Megan's clothes were stolen and it helps us a lot."

"Excuse me?" Mom says.

"Oh, I gave Megan some of my clothes," I interrupt, feeling my throat fall into my stomach like a lumpy rock sinking into the ocean.

"Oh—I'm sorry, you didn't know?" Megan's mom says.

"No, I didn't," Mom says, looking down at me.

"Oh, wow—I'm so embarrassed. I apologize. I'll have Megan return them tomorrow."

"No, no—that's okay. Please keep them," Mom says, patting the air.

"Are you sure?" Megan's mom asks.

"Positive."

"Thank you very much, we're really struggling." Megan's mom starts to cry.

"Go play." Mom shoos me off like a gnat flying over pizza. Megan and I walk to the monkey bars.

"I thought you asked your mom," Megan says.

"No! That's why I put the clothes in my backpack."

"But you said you did," Megan says. Thinking back, I clearly remember telling Megan I was *going* to ask my mom.

"No—I said I was going to ask her, but then she was late picking me up, remember?"

"Oh." Megan says.

"I'm gonna be in sooooo much trouble," I say, feeling the flood waters banging against the Hoover Dam.

"Sorry, I didn't know." We both look over at our moms. My mom is hugging her mom in the shade.

"What did Mr. Suarez tell you?" I ask.

"Just that we're supposed to tell."

"He told me the same thing," I say.

"Why did you tell Mrs. Washington?"

"Because I'm sick of Tera making fun of us," I say.

"But I thought you were friends with her." Mom is on her cell phone. She hands the phone to Megan's mom.

"What do you think they're talking about?" I ask. Megan shrugs.

"Well, I'm glad I told Mrs. Washington," I blurt out. Megan puts her backpack down and jumps up to climb the monkey bars. I follow behind her.

"Joanna!" Mom calls. The blacktop is crowded, with two long lines. Mom gives me five dollars because the PTA is selling strawberry smoothies. I buy one for me and one for Megan. Mom and Megan's mom are sitting next to the slide talking.

"This is so good," Megan slurps.

"I know, right?" When I pull the straw out it sounds like an oboe. I lick the dripping smoothie before it falls on my shirt.

"Whoa, brain freeze," Megan laughs. The clouds have moved and the sun is now melting my smoothie into strawberry syrup. Megan takes off her new sweater and folds it, placing it carefully into her backpack.

"Let's go, girls," Mom says. Megan and I squeeze each other's hands. She's coming home with us.

Memory Verse 11

1 Peter 5:7

"Give all your worries to him, because he cares for you."

Megan's mom, Ms. Stacy, has a blue SUV. I'm glad we don't have to walk to Ms. Karyn's house, because it's so hot it feels like the sun is shooting invisible lava on us. Our car looks so rusty and old that if it could talk it would say, *"I'm so old, Jurassic Park brought back memories."*

"Can I show Megan my room?" I ask Mom. I know it's not exactly *my* room, but I can still show her all of my stuff.

"You guys don't want a snack?" Mom asks. Megan and I look at each other and decide we don't. Mom, Ms. Karyn, and Ms. Stacy are talking in the living room and it's kind of awkward being downstairs. Upstairs, Emily is lying across the bed with a red bow.

"Is that your doll?" Megan asks. I hold my breath. It's like I'm in outer space and my space helmet somehow fell off. *"Houston—we have a problem."* What if Megan thinks I'm a baby for having a doll?

"She's so pretty!" Megan picks up Emily. My astronaut partner finds my helmet floating next to an asteroid and now I can breathe again.

"Thanks, I bought her last year for Christmas."

"Your bed is really comfy," Megan says, bouncing on the bed.

"It's actually not my bed. My mom lost her job, so we had to move out and move in with my mom's friend from church. I used to have my own room and everything. We put all the stuff from our old house in storage." I wish Megan could have seen *my* room.

"We have to live in a motel, but we used to live in our car," Megan says.

"You lived in your car? Where did you sleep? How did you take a shower?" Megan's braiding Emily's hair.

"We went to shelters sometimes, but we didn't live in the car that long."

"Where did you park the car? What did you do with all of your stuff?"

"We parked sometimes at the bus station, but only at night because they have security and if they caught us they'd make us move."

"So where do you live now?"

"Well, right now we don't really have a place to live, so we sleep at the motel."

"Why?" I ask. Mom would say it's rude to order the "gossip steak" when you could order the "none of your business salad," but I don't think it's gossip because I'm not going to tell anyone.

"It's a long story," Megan says, looking down.

"Oh." I probably should have stuck with the "none of your business salad," but I have so many questions, like "What's it like to live in a motel?", and "Do you get to order room service every day?"

"You have Apples to Apples!" Megan leaps off the bed like a frog, and frogs can jump over 20 times their own body length. I don't like playing Apples to Apples unless there are more people playing, but since Megan's so excited about it I sit on the floor with her. Megan hands me five red cards then places a green card between us. The green card says CRUNCHY. My cards are SPINACH, SAND CASTLES, PICKLES, HOT DOGS, and MY FEET.

"Since there's just the two of us, I don't think we need to put the cards on the floor face down," I say as I put the MY FEET card next to the green card.

"Your feet?" Megan asks. She pushes her pouty lips to the right side of her mouth, making her right cheek inflate like a balloon.

"Yeah," I laugh, raising my foot towards Megan. Megan squirms and squeals as I wiggle my crunchy feet.

"Okay, okay, stop!" She laughs.

"It's your turn," I remind her. Megan chooses HAIR.

"Hair, Megan? Really?" I tug gently on Megan's blonde and brown hair. Her roots are brown, but the ends are blonde.

"My hair gets really crunchy if I put a lot of hairspray in it. One time my mom put so much hairspray in my hair it felt like a porcupine." I hear my mom calling us so we throw our cards on the floor and skip down the stairs. Ms. Karyn has made nachos for us.

"Yum!" Megan says. The hyena boys are already eating. We wash our hands then sit at the big table. Megan's mom and my mom stand behind us.

"Did you say grace?" Mom asks. My mouth is dripping with nacho cheese sauce. I close my eyes and thank God for the food.

"I love nachos," Megan says, tilting her head to the side the way you do if a doctor is looking in your ear. She lets the cheese sauce dribble into her mouth.

"Why do you eat like that?" D'mari says.

"Because she wants to," I say back.

"Hey." Mom taps my shoulder, but D'mari is laughing at the way Megan eats her nachos. Ugh! The hyena boys think everything is funny.

"What's your name?" Krishawn asks. He's six.

"Megan," Megan says.

"My name is Krishawn. Are you gonna live with us?" The hyena boys are suddenly quiet and still, like we're playing freeze tag and they just got frozen.

"Yes, they are," Mom says. Megan and I look at each other out of the corner of our eyes.

"But where am *I* going to sleep?" Krishawn asks.

"We have to move your bunk bed into *my* room." D'mari answers like he's mad. I can't believe Megan is going to be living with us too! It's going to be so much fun—just like having a sister. I wonder which room Megan and her mom are going to sleep in. Hopefully in the room right next door to our room. The hyena boys are probably all going to have to share a room.

Megan's mom hugs her and kisses her cheek. I'm so glad we moved in with Ms. Karyn and Mr. Earl. They are so

64

nice to let Megan and her mom live with them too.

"Joanna, come upstairs with me," Mom says. I look for Megan, but she's busy talking to her mom. My heart sounds like a bongo player is performing a solo in my chest. If you slap two metal coffee cans really fast you can hear it. Mom closes the door as I sit on the bed. She exhales and sits down on the bed beside me.

"Mr. Suarez told me he talked to you today."

"He did?" I ask. Mom nods.

"Mmmhmmm…" My nails are so short from peeling them off I don't have any nails left.

"Why didn't you tell me?" Mom says, just like I knew she would.

I shrug my shoulders. "I don't know."

"You can always talk to me, especially if something is going on at school. I'm a little worried you didn't feel you could talk to me."

"Well—" The game show host is back. "*Ladies and gentlemen, let's welcome Joanna back to our show. The last time she was here she chose door number one. Which door will she pick this time?*"

"Well what, ladybug?" Mom asks.

"*Will Joanna tell her mother the real reason why she didn't tell her that she was always worried? And angry.*" The crowd boos. A lady in the audience wearing a red wig stands up and shouts, "*Don't do it! Joanna, you'll just get in more trouble!*" The spotlight is back on me, and the game show host, who is wearing a circus ringmaster costume, waves the microphone towards his mouth. "*Or will she say nothing and still get in trouble?*" The crowd boos again. *"Well Joanna, what's it gonna be?"*

"I just didn't want you to be more worried. You already have enough things to worry about."

Mom wraps her arms around me.

"Listen to me; nothing is more important to me than you. If something is going on at school I want to know about it because you are important to me."

"But it seems like every time I try to tell you something you get mad."

"Like what?" Mom says, getting mad.

"I don't know," I say. *"I told you not to choose door number one!"* the red wig lady shouts.

"Tell me, you're not in trouble," Mom says. *"Yes you are!"* the red wig lady says.

"I tell you about things sometimes like when I was thirsty when we were walking home and you got mad."

"Joanna, listen. Just because I get upset sometimes doesn't mean I don't love you or you can't come to me. Things have been a little crazy lately, but they're getting better."

"Okay," I say.

"Now, I understand why you gave Megan the clothes, but I'm sure you understand why you should have asked me first."

"I know. I just wanted to help her. Someone stole her underwear and Tera kept making fun of her."

"I understand, believe me I do. When I was growing up, I was bullied because I didn't have a lot of clothes."

"You were?"

"Yeah and a really nice girl did something I'll never forget. It was winter in Kentucky and I was walking home from school shivering 'cause it was freezing and I didn't have a sweater. A nice girl took off her sweater and gave it to me. That's why I'm very proud of you. You did a beautiful thing for Megan, but it was important that you talked to me first so that we could have gotten permission from her mother. But you already know that," Mom says, giving me a firm look.

"Sorry," I say.

"I also want you to tell me if things aren't changing with Tera and Riley." How does she know about Riley? Maybe Megan told Mr. Suarez.

"I don't understand why she treats people like that." I feel myself getting angry.

"I'm going to tell you what my mother told me: 'Hurting people hurt others.' That doesn't mean I'm making excuses, because it's not okay, that's for sure, but you can pray for Tera and Riley and treat them the way you want to be treated. I'm glad that you let Mrs. Washington know what was going on, because like I said, that kind of behavior is not okay."

I haven't thought about praying for Tera because I've been so mad. I wish Megan and I didn't have to go back to school and Ms. Karyn could teach us at home too. I don't want to see Tera or Riley ever again after what happened today, and I KNOW they definitely don't want to see me.

"So, as you heard, Ms. Karyn and Mr. Earl have decided to let Megan and her mother live here too."

"I know. I'm so happy!"

"Well, if my job interview went as well as I think it did, then we won't be staying here too much longer."

"But we just got here," I whine, making Mom laugh.

"I'm sure the boys would like to have their room back. I'm glad you like it here though."

Like it? I love it! No chores.

"I want you to start helping with the dishes and I want to see you doing your homework as soon as you get home."

"Yes, ma'am. And Mom?"

"Yes, ladybug."

"Thanks for getting Emily back for me."

"That was a no-brainer. There was no way Emily could stay in the house by herself." Mom leans over and whispers in my ear. "She's afraid of the dark."

I put my hands on my hips. "Oh really?" Mom laughs and opens her arms.

"Alright, give me a hug and get started on your homework." Mom squeezes me then tickles me.

"Hey!" she says as I run to the door.

"Yes?"

"Why didn't tell me you're the star student of the month?"

Memory Verse 12

Psalm 27:1
"Lord, you are my Light and my Savior,
so why should I be afraid of anyone?
The Lord is where my life is safe,
so I will be afraid of no one!"

Megan's mom, Ms. Stacy, gives us a ride to school. Megan and I didn't talk about Tera and Riley last night, but I can tell by the silence in the car that we're both thinking about what's going to happen. Ms. Stacy gives both of us a hug, then we line up on the blacktop because the bell has already rung. Tera's mom is walking with Tera toward the line and I pretend not to see them. I've never seen Tera's mom in the morning before. Out of the corner of my eye, I see Tera pointing at me. Tera's mom hands her an envelope and Tera walks over to me.

"Here." Tera shoves the envelope in my face. I take it and look straight ahead. A lady with curly brown hair and black glasses stands in front of our line.

"I think we have a substitute today," Lilia whispers. I stare at the envelope. I don't want to open it while Tera and her mom are watching me.

"What's that?" Megan says.

"I don't know," I shrug. The substitute's name is Ms. Kelly. She has three cats named Huey, Dewey, and Louie, and she loves the beach. Ms. Kelly has no idea that Tera and Riley hate me. When I get to my desk I can see Tera texting while Ms. Kelly sits at Mrs. Washington's desk. I put the envelope in my backpack and try to focus on the warm-up math problems in front of me. Riley is texting too and giggling. I bet they're talking about me.

Recess doesn't feel the same because Megan and I both feel like the thick "Tera" air is strangling us. "What's in the envelope?" Megan asks as we walk around the blacktop.

"I dunno, I didn't open it." Tera, Riley, and Lilia are in a circle looking at us and laughing, and Tera is putting her arm around Lilia the way she used to put it around me.

"Why not?" Megan says. I imagine myself wearing a black trench coat, dark sunglasses, a mustache, a black spy hat, and black pants and sitting on a park bench.

"Agent double-o-eight, do you have the cookie?" a voice coming from my watch says. I speak into my watch, *"Yes,"* I say through a small slit in my mouth. *Has the cookie been… baked?"* the worried voice asks. I look around the park to make sure no one is listening, raise my spy watch up to my cheek, and scratch my eyebrow.

"No. Not yet, there were too many people watching me."

"Good. The duck flies at midnight. Wait until then—and agent? Be careful," the voice orders.

"I will…Special agent double-o-eight over and out."

"Joanna? The bell rang," Megan says. Ms. Kelly, our substitute, lets us switch desks for reading groups because everyone told her that's what Mrs. Washington lets us do, even though she doesn't. I move to where Megan's desk is;

Tera, Riley, Lilia, Jake, and Evan sit together. Riley is sitting in my desk. When Ms. Kelly needs someone to take some papers to the office she asks me, since I'm the star student of the month. I see Mr. Suarez in the hallway.

"Hi Joanna," he smiles.

"Hi."

"Everything going okay?" he asks.

"Yeah," I say, smiling back.

"Good to hear." He pats my back and whistles down the hallway. The office lady takes the papers and lets me have a piece of sour apple candy from a bowl on her desk.

Back in class, Ms. Kelly wants us to get back to our "normal" desks because someone told. When I put my reading book back, I see a folded piece of paper hanging out of my desk. The paper says in big bold letters:

WHY IS JOANNA SO UGLY?
1. HER HAIR
2. HER TEETH
3. HER CLOTHES
4. HER SHOES

I look up at Tera then Riley and they're both staring at Ms. Kelly with serious looks on their face. My body feels like it's full of stingray venom. The pain is sharp and I think my heart is swelling. I ball up the paper and stuff it back in my desk. Megan is listening to Ms. Kelly explain our history lesson. She doesn't know I might throw up any minute. I raise my hand.

"Yes?"

"Can I use the bathroom?" I ask.

"Remember, I just said, if you have to use the bathroom you don't have to ask; you may just go."

"Oh." I take the envelope out of my backpack and slip it under my shirt, then I speed walk into the bathroom. The bathroom is empty, but someone must have just left because the water is still running. I go into the bathroom stall and take the envelope from underneath my shirt. It's sealed closed. What if there are worms inside it? Or poison. Tera hates me so much there's no telling what could be inside of the envelope. It doesn't smell weird—actually, it doesn't have a smell at all. There's no writing on the front or the back. It's just a plain white envelope. If it is poisonous I probably shouldn't open it by myself in the bathroom.

Opening the stall door, I stare at my teeth in the mirror. I still have a lot of my baby teeth. Maybe that's why Tera or Riley said my teeth are ugly. Mom twisted my hair using three-strand twists and I think it looks really nice, even though they think it's ugly. My clothes are old, and I haven't gotten any new shoes in a really long time; my shoes are dirty and the plastic part on the shoestring is gone so the shoestrings are coming apart. When my shoes were new they weren't ugly, but that was during Christmas break.

The trashcan is covered in wet and dry paper towel balls. I could throw the envelope away, but our janitor Mr. Felix might find it and think the poison or whatever is inside the envelope was meant for him, and he's really nice. Maybe I should wet the envelope in the sink, rip it up into tiny pieces, and *then* throw it away. I turn the faucet on and the door opens. It's a girl named Rachel from my class.

"Ms. Kelly wanted me to check on you; we're leaving for specials," she says, looking down at the envelope.

"Okay," I say, waiting for her to leave.

"Are you coming?" What am I supposed to do with the envelope now!

"Yeah in just a minute, my stomach hurts. I think I need to go back to the bathroom," I groan.

"Okay, I'll tell Ms. Kelly you'll meet us in the music room." If Mrs. Washington were here she would send me to the nurse's office, but maybe Ms. Kelly won't mind if I walk to music by myself. Rachel finally leaves and I turn the water back on. Then two more girls come into the bathroom. Now I can't even rip up the envelope, so I go into the bathroom stall. It stinks really bad, and there are noises I don't want to hear, so I put the envelope back under my shirt and run out of the bathroom where I can breathe again. My entire class is walking towards me. I join the line.

"Why are you holding your stomach like that?" Megan whispers while our music teacher Mr. Ward picks Jake to pass out the recorders. I lift my shirt high enough for Megan to see the envelope.

"What's inside it?" Megan asks.

"I don't know. I didn't open it yet," I say, cupping my hand over Megan's ear.

"Still?"

"Yeah, it might be poisonous."

Megan giggles. "It's not poisonous. Do you want me to open it?"

"No, I'll open it after school." Megan nods because Mr.

Ward is staring at us the way Mrs. Washington does when she's taking her "mental notes" of who's not listening. We're learning a new song today. When I play the recorder, it sounds like the recorder is screaming for help.

"Don't curve your fingers, Joanna," Mr. Ward says. He holds his recorder in the air.

"Use your finger pads and you'll get a nice sound." It works. I cover the holes with my fingers flat, and I start playing much better.

In the cafeteria Tera, Riley, and Lilia are sitting together laughing and whispering. I pull out my lunch. Ms. Karyn let Megan and me make our own lunches this morning. Megan made a peanut butter and jelly sandwich and I made a roast beef sandwich with mayo, lettuce, and tomatoes.

"Just ignore them," Megan says, taking a bite of her sandwich.

"I'm trying." I take a drink of my apple juice.

"Did you bring the envelope?"

"No, I put it in my backpack after specials."

"We can open it together after school if you want," Megan says.

"I was thinking about throwing it away."

"Why?" Megan asks. I don't want to tell her about the note. Every time I think about it the Hoover Dam gets a new crack. If I talk about it, the dam might break completely.

"I don't know."

"If you're worried it's something bad, I'll open it for you. If there's something bad inside then *I'll* throw it away and we never have to talk about it, but if it's something good

74

I'll give it to you."

"Okay." I take another bite of my sandwich.

In class, I sneak Megan the envelope. It feels like I'm handing her a heavy brick. The clock is moving too fast, I wish I could freeze time so Megan never has to open the envelope, but she does on the way out to the blacktop. Tera and Riley are busy playing games on their cell phones and Ms. Kelly doesn't seem to mind. Megan and I agreed that Megan would line up at the end of the line and I would line up in the front so I don't cheat and peek. I have no idea what Megan is looking at.

"Well?" I whisper to Megan in the backseat of her mom's SUV.

"I think it's good," Megan says in a high-pitched voice, like she's asking me a question.

"Why do you *think* it's good? How come you don't *know* it's good?"

"Because—I think it's a good thing, but I just don't know what it means," Megan says.

"What do you mean?"

"Here, I'll just show you." Megan reaches inside her backpack and pulls out the envelope.

Memory Verse 13

1 Peter 4:8

"Most important of all, love each other deeply, because love makes you willing to forgive many sins."

My fingers slip under the fold of the envelope and I pull out a note. It says in cursive: "Buy your own bikini." The gift card Mom bought for Tera's birthday is inside the envelope, unopened.

"What does it mean?" Megan asks. I should have ripped it up and thrown it away. I never should have let Megan open it. A rush of raging waters full of sharp rocks has destroyed the Hoover Dam.

"I'm sorry. Please don't cry. I'm sorry. I didn't know it was bad." Megan's voice is shaky.

"What's going on back there?" Ms. Stacy asks.

"Please don't tell, please? I didn't know," Megan starts to cry too.

"It's okay, it's my fault, Megan. You're not in trouble. I borrowed Tera's bikini at her birthday party."

"Hello? Girls? Megan, what's going on?" Ms. Stacy says more loudly. Her eyes are studying me in the rear view mirror.

"Tera gave Joanna a mean gift," Megan says.

"What do you mean a mean gift?" Ms. Stacy asks.

"And a mean note," Megan says, rubbing my back.

"Why would Tera give you a gift with a mean note, Joanna?" I tell Ms. Stacy everything I know, including the part where I borrowed Tera's bikini at her swim party even though Mom told me I could only wear a one-piece.

"You know, this Tera girl has been bothering Megan all year, and it's sad to see that her mother would do something like that," Ms. Stacy says. Back at Ms. Karyn's house, Ms. Stacy and Mom talk privately downstairs while Megan and I talk privately upstairs.

"I never should have gone to Tera's party, especially when she was being so mean to you."

"It's okay, if Tera would have invited me, I would have done the same thing," Megan says, trying to make me feel better, but I know she wouldn't have. Megan is better than me because even though I hung out with Tera, Megan still wanted to be friends with me. Megan forgave me as if I did nothing wrong.

"Are you going to tell Mr. Suarez?" Megan asks.

"I don't know," I sigh, holding Emily. Mom comes in and asks Megan to go downstairs to do homework.

"Hey ladybug," Mom says, sitting beside me.

"Hey."

"You know I wish I could tell you you're always going to get along with everyone, but I can't."

"Why do Tera and her mom hate me so much? All I did was tell Tera to stop making fun of Megan."

"Let's start focusing on who loves you. You know I love you with all of my heart, but God loves you even more and it makes Him sad to see you sad. I know it's hard and it really hurts your feelings that you and Tera aren't friends, but you stood up for Megan and that was the right thing to do because it shows other kids that they can stand up too."

"I didn't always stand up for Megan, Mom," I confess.

"Well, it's not an easy thing to do. One day when I was at work, I was sitting in the lunchroom, and one of my co-workers started saying not-so-nice things about my friend Ms. Lisa. I didn't say anything to my co-worker because I was afraid I would offend her. The entire day I felt really bad about the fact I didn't speak up. The next day we had a meeting and my coworker complained about Ms. Lisa and she said I agreed with her. I couldn't blame her for thinking that, even though it wasn't the truth, because I had sat silently. Believe me, it's much easier to just go with the flow and stay silent, just like it's easier to stay angry with Tera than it is to forgive her and pray for her."

"It's *so* hard, Mom. I want to hate her, but I still want her to be my friend."

"What if you decided to do the same things to her that she did to you and Megan do you think you would feel better?"

"Probably yeah," I admit.

"Really?" Mom raises her eyebrows.

"Mom, you don't know. She looks at me and laughs at me the entire day. She makes me hate school, and yesterday I found a really mean note in my desk that said, 'Why is Joanna so ugly?'"

"I'm sorry, honey," Mom takes my hand.

"I think it was Riley, because she was sitting at my desk,

but I don't know for sure. Every time I see them whispering and laughing at me, it feels like someone scratched my skin and it's bleeding," I say. Since the Hoover Dam is broken now, I can let the water flow down my face. Mom nods and wipes the water away with her thumb.

"I know it's tough to love people when they hurt us, but that's exactly what Jesus taught. It doesn't mean that we excuse their behavior by pretending it's not happening, because it is important to let someone know what's going on. But what it *does* mean is that we need to look at them through new eyes; eyes that show us why we need to forgive them, eyes that show us why we should pray for them, and eyes that show us how we can show God's love. We may not see them change with our eyes but we will see the change in our hearts."

"Do you think Tera will change?" I ask.

"Keep praying for her, ladybug, and when the opportunity presents itself, choose to be kind. And remember that God loves Tera and her mom just as much as He loves you and me, right?" Mom says. I realize she thinks I've been praying for Tera all this time, but all I've been thinking about is how much she hates me.

"Yes ma'am," I say.

"Thank you for telling me, honey, I know it's hard to talk about." Mom has no idea how hard it is for me to talk about it, but I do feel better.

I decide it's time to pray for Tera. I close my eyes at the same time Mom closes the door.

Dear God,

I probably should have talked to you about Tera sooner, but I was so mad. I really need new eyes so I can see Tera the way you see her. How DO you see her? I want her to be my friend, but if she can't be a friend can you please give her new eyes too? Also, can you please give Riley new eyes too? And one more thing, I don't know how I can be nice to her when she's so mean to me so I would appreciate any ideas. Thanks for helping me.

In Jesus' Name

Amen

***

Mom wants to wait with me on the blacktop in case Tera's mom has another envelope. When I see Tera, she cuts in line to stand next to Lilia. Mrs. Washington is still not back, but Ms. Kelly is here and she's nice too.

"Have a good day," Mom waves. I wave goodbye and walk behind Megan to our class. Today is my first day as a time traveler. I'm wearing an aviator helmet and pilot goggles because I'm traveling back in time to when Tera and I were friends. My goggles allow me to see her smile (even though she's really giving me a mean look) and I can even hear her laughing with me instead of at me.

"Time for reading groups," Ms. Kelly says.

"Can we switch desks again?" Lilia asks.

"Sure," Ms. Kelly answers. It's like the day really *is* starting over. Taking out my notebook I tear out a piece of paper and write a note to the person who is going to leave a mean note in my desk. It says:

Why do I want to be friends with you?

1. You're really fun

2. You can be a nice friend

3. I miss being friends with you

I sit next to Megan. Riley, Tera, and Lilia sit together again. Ms. Kelly asks me if I will take the attendance to the office.

"Sure," I say. This time Tera is sitting at my desk. In the front office, the office lady with red hair gives me another sour apple candy. So far going back in time is pretty awesome. Reading groups take forever to finish, but finally the timer goes off. I glance at Tera and then at Riley. They don't seem to notice a time traveler in the room. Maybe they can see the old me, but not the new me. Slowly, I bend my head down and look inside of my desk. The note is gone.

Memory Verse 14

Phil. 1:12

"Brothers and sisters, I want you to know that all that has happened to me has helped to spread the Good News."

"I thought you were my friend," Tera says, with her hands on her hips. Lilia and Riley are standing beside her with their arms folded on their chests. Ms. Kelly is busy talking to another teacher and Megan went to the nurse's office because she's not feeling good. It's just me and the three of them in the open field with Tera's angry eyes. Her face is as red as a tomato.

"I only told Mrs. Washington because Megan is *my* friend."

Tera switches from leaning on one leg to the other.

"You were making fun of her too!" Tera's mouth is moving so fast she spits in my face.

"No, I wasn't," I say as Tera moves closer to my face.

"Yes you were, Joanna, don't lie," she commands.

"When?" My voice is shaking. When will the recess bell ring?

"You were laughing too—it wasn't just me, Joanna. Remember in class? And if you were so tired of it, then why did you come to my party? Why did you borrow my bathing suit? Why did you pretend to be my best friend?" Tera sounds really upset, as if I did something wrong. But I never made fun of Megan. I never said anything about Megan. Then I hear Mom's voice whispering in my ear, *"I told you ladybug, saying nothing can sometimes make people think you agree with what they're saying."*

"Why?" Tera pushes. "Answer me!"

"I—wanted to be your friend," I say. I never should have agreed to meet Tera on the field, but I wanted to know what she was going to say.

"I thought you were my friend, but you got me in so much trouble," Tera says with tears in her eyes.

"It's okay, Tera," Riley says, putting her arm around Tera. Lilia looks down at the ground and the bell still hasn't rung.

"I didn't want to get you in trouble. I just wanted you to stop making fun of Megan."

"Then why didn't you just ask me? Why did you have to tell Mrs. Washington and Mr. Suarez? I was just kidding. I wasn't even being serious. I make fun of Riley all the time, but she's knows I'm just messing around, she doesn't go tell everybody," Tera says looking at Riley."

Just kidding? She used to make me cry every day, but she was only kidding?

"I don't want to fight with you, Tera, but I don't think you were just kidding and if you were it wasn't funny. You really hurt Megan's feelings and you used to make me cry all the time." Tera squeezes her cheeks with her hands.

"Oh my gosh, Joanna! Then *why* were you trying to be

my friend?" She growls through her teeth.

"Girls! Come in!" Ms. Kelly waves.

"My mom told me that some girls are fake and they just use you for what you have because they're jealous. You shouldn't be jealous of what other people have. Maybe if you had nice things you wouldn't act so fake," Tera snaps. Riley and Lilia follow Tera off the field. Nothing like this has ever happened to me before. I'm too embarrassed to walk and I'm too angry to cry so I'm just standing here. I don't understand. I tried being nice to her, I prayed for her, and I told her the truth about wanting to be her friend.

"Joanna!" Ms. Kelly calls. The bell has just rung. With Megan gone, I won't have anyone to sit with at lunch. Maybe Tera is right. Maybe I should have told her how I felt, because now Tera thinks I betrayed *her* and I'm jealous of her. The day goes by slowly. All day I wonder if things will ever get better.

When I get home to Ms. Karyn's house, I find out that Megan has a cold and she's spending the entire day in bed. Mom is on the phone upstairs with the person she had an interview with, so Ms. Karyn helps me with my homework. "How are things going?" she asks. She has a warm voice like hot cocoa on a chilly day.

"Ok," I say.

"Just ok? Can I tell you something?"

"Sure," I say, putting my pencil down.

"I would love for you to come with me this weekend to volunteer. I'm going to get up early in the morning and make us a nice breakfast. Would you like to come with me?" Ms.

Karyn asks. Her eyes have smile lines right above her cheeks. I don't like getting up early, but I love Ms. Karyn's breakfasts.

"Yes ma'am," I say.

"Good, that's real good. You finish your homework and then you can help me make my famous honey-lemon tea for Megan," she says.

Mom comes downstairs just as I finish my homework. She looks really pretty, her hair is curled, and she's wearing a navy blue dress.

"Oh Ladybug, God is so good!" she says, squeezing me.

"Did you get the job?" Ms. Karyn asks.

"I sure did," she says.

"Congratulations!" Ms. Karyn rushes to Mom and hugs us both.

"They offered me the job on the spot," Mom says.

"I think we need to celebrate. How about I order pizzas?" Ms. Karyn says.

"Pizza!" D'mari jumps in the air.

"Ms. Karyn is going to take me with her to volunteer," I tell Mom.

"How exciting."

"When do you start your new job?" I ask. Mom's face is shining so bright her eyes twinkle. She takes off her high-heeled shoes and tosses them to the floor.

"Next week. I'm working the same hours I did before, so you'll get to go to Safe Zone before and after school."

"Can we still live here?" I ask, even though I already

know the answer. Maybe Mom will think about how much I love living with Megan. Megan and I were planning on going swimming in Ms. Karyn's pool all summer long, and the hyena boys have finally stopped laughing at everything I say and do.

"No honey," Mom says, pushing my hair away from my face. "You've been so patient and I know you miss having your own room." One thing I like about Ms. Karyn's house is that it's like we're one big family. Since my grandma died and all of my cousins and aunts and uncles live in either Kentucky or Mississippi, we don't have any family in Las Vegas. Our house was so quiet compared to Ms. Karyn's house. Plus I love all the arts and crafts we make. Ms. Karyn is even going to teach Megan and me how to sew. Emily loves it here too. She's never afraid, because there's always a light on in the house.

"Maybe we can find a house on the same street." I've noticed a lot of "for sale" signs in the neighborhood.

"Don't worry, we're going to visit all the time," Mom says. Megan's coughing in the next room reminds me I need to help Ms. Karyn make her honey-lemon tea. I'm so glad it's Friday and tomorrow I'll be somewhere that helps me take my mind off of the things Tera said.

"Have you worked on your star student poster?" Mom asks. I had forgotten all about it. I'm going to have to present soon and I have no idea what I'm going to talk about.

"Well, you better get started," Mom says, opening the drawer beside the bed. She pulls out the star student paper she must have found in my backpack and reads it to me. It says:

Dear Family,

Your child has been chosen to be our class super star student for the month! This is an exciting event in our classroom. Your child was chosen because they have demonstrated excellent manners, a positive attitude, and a dedication to learning.

To celebrate, please fill out the super star student form as soon as possible. In addition to this form, please send in 5–8 pictures of your child. The questionnaire and pictures will be displayed in the classroom,

Sincerely, Mrs. Washington

All about: <u>Joanna</u> (please describe your child using the letters of their name)

J- oy she is a joy

O- utstanding. She is an outstanding person.

A- nimals. She has so much love and compassion for animals.

N-ice I am proud that she is nice to others.

N- ot afraid to speak up. She is brave and speaks up for others.

A-wesome. She is an awesome daughter to have.

"YOU" (Please write your child a short note using the letter "You") example: **You** are great.

Dear Joanna,

I am proud of **you** for being **you**. Your light shines bright and **you** always make me smile. **You** are valuable. I'm grateful for you. **You** matter.

I Love **you.**

Memory Verse 15

Nehemiah 8:10

"Nehemiah said, "Go and enjoy the good food and sweet drinks. Give some food and drinks to those who didn't prepare any food. Today is a special day to our Lord. Don't be sad, because the joy of the Lord will make you strong."

Ms. Karyn cooks a ham and cheese omelet for breakfast and my favorite—tater tots. I love tater tots, but Ms. Karyn's are the best because they're homemade. The sun squirms through the clouds. It seems like only a few minutes have passed as Ms. Karyn parks in the church parking lot that says "reserved."

"Alright, we're here, ready Freddy?" Ms. Karyn asks.

"Yes ma'am" I answer. The normally crowded sidewalks are silent; there are no "CLICK-CLACK" sounds from high heels or "PLOP-PLOPS" from sandals. We pass by the church bookstore, where they sell pencils, cool erasers, bookmarks, t-shirts, and of course lots of books, then we pass the main church building where the adults have church. The kids have a treehouse-looking building that is sorted by grade level and a big slide that connects to the playground below. Mom never lets me take the slide down even though all the other kids do.

"Good morning!" a lady with blonde hair and sparkling green eyes says. She gives Ms. Karyn a hug.

"I brought a new helper with me." Ms. Karyn pulls me closer to her.

"I see that, so nice to have you here this morning." She smells like freshly baked chocolate chip cookies.

"Thank you." I really want a cookie. Looking around the room, I see brown bags lined up on rows of tables, but no cookies! Where are the cookies? Ms. Karyn gives me a handful of index cards. She explains that whatever is on the index cards is what needs to go into each brown linen bag.

"The supplies are over here," she says, pointing to the supply cabinets. There are all kinds of things in the cabinets, like mini toothbrushes, toothpaste, mouthwash, socks, Bibles, and water bottles to name a few, but I don't see any cookies and my stomach is getting impatient.

"Who are the bags for?"

"These are 'need' bags. People can write what they need and we fill the bags with what we have." Ms. Karyn tells me she will be helping Ms. Jessica next door to fill the bigger "need" bags with canned food. It reminds me of when Mom and I needed food and we went to the food pantry. I had no idea our church gave away food and supplies. I don't think Mom knows either.

More kids walk through the door to volunteer. They seem to know exactly what to do, because they grab their index cards and get right to work.

"Hi, I'm Sophia," says a girl who looks close to my age.

"I'm Joanna." I put some toothpaste into the bag.

"I've never seen you here before," Sophia says.

"It's my first time here."

"I come every week. It's a lot of fun, plus when we're done helping, Jessica gives us cookies and they're so yummy." I knew it! The nose knows…

"Cool," I say. Sophia moves so fast I can hardly keep up, but we fill every bag. The bigger kids that are here help us move the bags into the auditorium next door. There are a lot of people in the auditorium now. Where did all these people come from? I see so many kids.

"How long have we been in there?" I ask.

Sophia glances at her cell phone. "It's eleven o'clock."

"Wow, I got here at ten."

"Would you like to help pass out the bags you made?" Ms. Karyn asks.

"Sure!" I join the line of volunteers behind the long tables and give the bags to the parents and backpacks filled with school supplies to the kids.

I hear a voice. I know that voice. I turn around and see a girl with long black braids. I can't believe it—it's Riley! Riley sees me at the same time I see her. By the look on her face, I think it takes a second for her brain to say, "I can't believe it, it's Joanna!"

"Hi Riley," I say, but she doesn't answer. She is staring at me with her mouth wide open.

"Riley? Do you hear her talking to you?" a lady I think is her mom says.

"Hi…" Riley mumbles. I turn around and examine the backpacks. There are some plain black ones, and blue ones, but I see a pretty sparkly purple backpack.

"Here you go." I hand Riley the backpack.

"What do you say?" says the lady she's with. Riley looks down.

"Thanks," she says, then turns her face away from me. I don't know for sure if she's crying, but I see her wiping her face.

"What's gotten into you? Huh? What's wrong with you?" The lady asks, yanking Riley away. I wish I could tell Riley that there's nothing to be embarrassed about, but she's already gone. Ms. Karyn and I join Ms. Jessica in the kitchen and pass out the cookies. I'm not exaggerating when I say this is the best chocolate chip cookie I have ever had in my entire life. The creamy chocolate melts in my mouth and the cookie is soft and chewy at the same time. How is that even possible?

"Ms. Jessica this cookie is ah-maze-zing," I say, because it really is.

"Why thank you, this is a family recipe. It's been in my family for many generations." I can totally see why. Ms. Jessica should win a trophy or something. If there was a best cookie award she would win first place and of course I would have to be one of the judges. I would pick up a cookie, take a bite and say, *"Hmmm…I need ten more cookies to make my final decision."*

"But you've already eaten thirty, Joanna," the other judges would say.

"Do you want me to pick a winner or not?" And then after I'd finished eating those cookies I would eat ten more. We get chocolate milk to go with our cookie and I feel like I'm floating on a happy cloud.

"Can I come with you every week?" I ask Ms. Karyn.

"Sure, if it's okay with your mom."

"Can I have one more cookie?" I ask, licking a crumb from my lip. If Mom was here she would tell me to *"save some for other people."*

"Absolutely, you did a fantastic job today," Ms. Karyn says. Sophia gives me her phone number just in case I want to hang out at her house sometime. Ms. Karyn saves the number in her cell phone for me.

Back at the house, Mom is talking to the mechanic. She looks like she could use one of Ms. Jessica's cookies. Fortunately, Ms. Karyn brought cookies home for everyone. Megan is still not feeling well. Her nose is so stuffy she can't even taste the cookie.

"Tell me again what it tastes like," she groans, then coughs. Poor Megan.

"It tastes like you're swimming in a chocolate river and you don't want to come up for air."

"Yum, like a Willy Wonka river?" she sneezes.

"Yep, just like a Willy Wonka river," I say, covering my nose and mouth. I don't want to get Megan's cold.

"Guess what?" I say, remembering that I saw Riley at the church. I can see the waiter with the curly mustache and the "Alfred" from Batman accent, holding the sizzling, juicy gossip steak.

"Your juicy gossip steak has arrived, Madame," he says. Megan's watery eyes brighten.

"What?" Her voice sounds like a harmonica with a cold. The steak is so tempting, so juicy, but what if Riley had seen me at the food pantry when I felt embarrassed? Now I know there's nothing to be embarrassed about, but I didn't feel that way back then.

"I'm going back next week, wanna come?" I say instead.

"*Sorry, but I ordered the silent salad,*" I tell the waiter. The waiter looks pretty mad.

"*We don't serve silent salad here; we only serve juicy gossip steak. You'll have to take your business elsewhere,*" the waiter says.

"*Fine! Your gossip steak doesn't look that juicy anyway.*"

"Yeah I wanna come! Hopefully I'll be able to smell again. Ms. Karyn is making meatloaf and mashed potatoes and green beans for dinner tonight, and my mom is making her famous potato salad. Will you tell me what everything tastes like?" Megan asks.

"My pleasure, my dear," I say in my best waiter's accent.

Memory Verse 16

Romans 8:28

"We know that in everything God works for the good of those who love him. These are the people God chose, because that was his plan."

Mrs. Washington has returned! She says she was sick with the flu, but she's feeling much better. She's reading the letter our substitute teacher Ms. Kelly left for her.

"Hmmm…," she says, looking down at the paper. The entire class is silent. Does it say that we switched desks during reading groups? Or we were talking without raising our hands? Mrs. Washington finally looks up and around the room.

"I am very pleased that Ms. Kelly has approved your pizza party." Pizza party? What pizza party?

"Whoo-hoo!" the class cheers, even though everyone knows we don't deserve a pizza party.

"Ms. Kelly said even though there were a few "hiccups," for the most part you were well-behaved and respectful and I appreciate that, so I am treating the class to a pizza party this Friday and we will watch a movie." So far today is awesome.

"We are trying something new for math warm-ups. We're going to work with a buddy. You and your buddy will

review the practice test since your math test is on Thursday."
Oh no! Megan is still home sick and I don't have anyone else
to partner with.

"I have chosen your partners," Mrs. Washington says,
reading my mind. I hope I get Rachel or Alaina. They're both
really smart and good in math, and math isn't my best
subject. When Mrs. Washington calls my name, I hold my
breath like I'm a diver exploring the warm, salty waters of
the Caribbean, with clownfish and angelfish swimming
beside me.

"Joanna and Riley," Mrs. Washington says. Riley makes
a face like she just bit into a moldy onion. She reaches into
her new purple backpack and pulls out a pencil. I grab my
mechanical pencil, math journal, and practice test and sit
next to Riley.

"Hey," I say, sitting down. Riley doesn't say anything.

"Are there any questions you don't get?" I ask, because
I'm confused on a lot of the math problems. We're learning
how to multiply fractions and I'm still struggling with
multiplication. Riley still doesn't answer.

"Hel-lo? " I wave my hand.

"Just do whatever you want," she says, already working
on the first problem.

"I didn't tell anyone about yesterday," I whisper. Riley
doesn't look at me.

"I don't hear enough talking," Mrs. Washington says,
walking around the room. I think this is the first time Mrs.
Washington has ever told us to talk.

"We need to work together, otherwise Mrs. Washington

is gonna get mad," I say.

"I don't care," Riley snaps. She's already finished with the first five problems and I still haven't finished one. I'm surprised Riley and Tera aren't texting about Riley being my math partner. Actually, I haven't seen Riley and Tera talk all morning, and they didn't stand next to each other in line.

"You're really fast. I don't get this at all," I say.

"It's easy," Riley mumbles.

"Maybe for you, but it's hard for me. English is my best subject. I hate math."

"I love math," Riley says.

"I wish I could love math, but it's just so confusing."

"You just have to find something you love and find the math in it," Riley says.

"Like what?"

"Like, I love cooking and there's a lot of math in cooking, so my grandma helps me learn math when I cook things. When I make cookies, I have to use fractions to measure flour and sugar."

"I love cookies. I had the best cookies this weekend. I brought some with me for lunch. Do you want one?" I ask. Mrs. Washington lets us eat a snack in class if we're really hungry. Riley shakes her head.

"Are you sure? They're really good."

"No," Riley says.

"How are you two doing?" Mrs. Washington asks as she walks by.

"Fine," I say.

"Ten more minutes," Mrs. Washington announces.

"So do you go to the church?" I ask.

"No."

"Oh. It's a nice church. They have small groups for fifth graders and during the summer we have a sleepover at church and we play games. It's really fun." Riley doesn't answer; she just keeps writing faster.

"I thought you wanted to know how to do this," Riley says.

"I do," I say. Riley puts down her pencil and explains the math problem using her pointer finger. I notice that Tera is staring at us. Riley sees her too, but she doesn't stop helping me.

"Three minutes," Mrs. Washington says, holding up three fingers.

"Do you want to come to my house and hang out sometime? Well—it's not exactly *my* house. I live with my mom's friend because my mom lost her job, but she has a new one now." Riley looks up at me again so I decide to keep talking.

"I don't have my own room, I share a room with my mom, but we can play Apples to Apples or I can ask my mom if we can swim in the pool since it's getting warmer now."

"Yeah, sure," Riley says. I can't believe it! I'm so excited. *Be cool, Joanna. Be cool.*

"Okay, ask your mom today."

"I live with my grandma," Riley says. She seems to be examining every word that comes out of my mouth as if the words are floating in the air.

"Back to your desks, journals away," Mrs. Washington orders. I can't wait to tell Megan the good news.

I don't mind that it's lunchtime, even though Megan's not here. I have Ms. Jessica's delicious cookies to keep me company. Tera's sitting with Lilia and Riley is sitting by herself. I don't know what happened, but whatever happened is the filet mignon of juicy gossip steaks.

"Hey, can I sit by you?" I ask Riley.

"If you want," she says. The waiter is back, holding a gold platter of buttery charbroiled filet mignon gossip steak. *"Your delicious buttery charbroiled filet mignon gossip steak has arrived, madam,"* the waiter says. It's so tempting! I just want to take a big bite and ask, *"So what happened between you and Tera?"* My mouth waters as I gaze at Tera and Lilia texting and laughing. The aroma fills my nose and I can taste the marvelous marinated mouthwatering melting meat sauce moistening the magnificent gossip.

"No thanks, I'll have the 'none of my business salad,'" I say to the waiter instead.

"For the last time, if you aren't going to eat our marvelously marinated mouthwatering melting meat sauce- moistening magnificent gossip, then you'll have to take your business elsewhere, because knowing other people's business is our business."

"Wanna cookie?" I open the sandwich baggie.

"Sure," Riley says. I can tell by the way her eyes get big that she loves the cookie.

"Good, huh?" I smile.

"Yeah, not bad."

"I'm sure you're wondering why I'm not siting with

Tera," Riley adds.

"*Who? Moi?*" I say in my best French accent. Riley laughs.

"It's because—"

"Wait!" I hold up my hand. "It's okay, you don't have to tell me, it's really none of my business."

"I'm just sick of her making fun of everybody all the time. She says she's 'just kidding' because she doesn't want to get in trouble, but she's not. I'm glad you told Mrs. Washington, but she's still doing it." Even though Riley doesn't say it, I know it hurts her feelings that Tera makes fun of her.

"Do you think your grandma will let you come over Saturday afternoon?"

"I'll ask." She slurps her chocolate milk.

"Cool, Megan's going to be so happy."

"Why?" Riley asks.

"Oh. Megan lives with us too," I say.

"She does?" Riley's eyebrows shoot to the top of her forehead like shooting stars. My face is tingling and my stomach feels like I'm on the "Dragon Fly" carnival ride.

"Yeah-I—" I hope Megan won't be mad I told Riley. She would find out anyway if Riley came over.

"You what?" Riley asks. *I don't know if I should have told you*, I wish I could say.

"It's a long story," I sigh. I'm sure Megan won't mind. I mean, she'll understand that I want to be friends with Riley and I don't want her to be embarrassed, won't she?

Saved by the bell. Riley snaps out of her staring contest

with Tera and she seems to have forgotten about Megan.

In class, Mrs. Washington loves the pictures Mom sent of me for the star student poster.

"Have you started working on your poster?" Mrs. Washington asks.

"Not yet..." I mutter.

"I want you to present on Monday," she says.

"This Monday coming up?"

"Yes ma'am." Great. I still have no idea what I'm going to talk about and now I have to come up with something by Monday. My life just got way more complicated.

Ms. Stacy picks me up from school since Mom's started her new job. Mom said I can't go to Safe Zone until we move. Back at home, Megan is finally looking like a human again; her nose is back to its normal color, her face isn't as swollen, and her eyes aren't teary.

"Guess what?" I say, pouncing on her bed.

"What?" Megan asks.

"I invited Riley over this weekend," I say. Megan's face goes from superhero happy to evil villain angry.

"What? You can't!"

"Meg-gan, keep it down. I haven't asked my mom yet."

"Why would you tell her?" Megan's voice is still raspy and deeper than normal.

"Because I don't care if she knows that Ms. Karyn is helping us. She was so embarrassed about the backpack thing and I want her to know she doesn't have to feel like that because sometimes people need help and there's nothing wrong with that."

"What backpack thing? And it's none of her business," Megan's voice cracks. Oops, I can see the waiter.

"Ahem? I believe the young lady asked, 'what backpack thing.'" Megan's so mad, hopefully she'll forget I mentioned it.

"She doesn't even talk to Tera anymore, if that's what you're worried about, and even if she did, I don't care. I'm not embarrassed that we're living here."

"I don't want her to know!" Whoa! I've never heard Megan yell.

"There's nothing to be embarrassed about." I can see Megan has built a Hoover Dam around her, because her lips are shaking, but her eyes are dry. I've never seen Megan this upset before. How can anyone be friends if everyone has a Hoover Dam?

Memory Verse 17

Colossians 3:15

'Let the peace that Christ gives control your thinking. It is
for peace that you were chosen to be together in one
body. And always be thankful."

Mom is tapping her nose with her pointer finger. Is she going to let Riley come over? I told her everything that happened with Riley, including the "backpack thing." Then I told her what Megan said, and she's been tapping her nose ever since. The suspense is worse than waiting for a new superhero movie to come out after you just finished watching the previews at the movie theater.

"Mom?"

"I'm thinking…" I thought moms were supposed to already know what to do in situations like this. Normally when I ask Mom what to do she either says *"Sure Joanna"* or *"No Joanna"* in less than five seconds. Mom finally stops tapping her nose.

"Well?"

"I'm going to let you handle this one," she says.

"Me? You can't let me handle it. I'm only ten. I have no idea what I should do. I can't make a decision like this."

"Sure you can." Mom stands up.

"You're supposed to say that I was wrong for inviting Riley over without talking to you first, and then you're supposed to say that if I want Riley to come over you have to talk to her grandma to make sure it's okay, but I still need to talk to Megan about it since Megan is so upset."

"Sounds like you've got it covered," Mom says, heading toward the door.

"Wait—you can't leave!" I hold my arms out to block the door.

"Why not?" Mom asks, putting her hands on her hips.

"Because you're my parent. You can't just leave it up to me. What if I bring a cow in the house to save it from getting hit by a school bus? Or what if I decide I want to eat candy for dinner?"

"Well, if you brought a cow in the house, we'd probably save a lot of money on milk, and how nice to save a cow from getting hit by a school bus. If you do decide to eat candy for dinner, I can't say that I blame you; candy is delicious, especially licorice. Now can I please go downstairs?"

"You're asking *me* for permission? This isn't funny. I really need you to tell me what I should do." I fold my arms across my chest.

"I trust your judgment and I like the sound of candy for dinner. I think Ms. Karyn has a secret stash in the cabinet downstairs. Now if you'll excuse me," Mom says, and just like that all of the responsibility falls on me.

The first thing I have to do is talk to Megan. Megan is doing her make-up homework downstairs. Since she's so mad, I have to find a way to make her smile, so I decide to wear Mom's fancy and very poufy pink bridesmaid dress she wore to my Aunt Nisha's wedding. I put on Mom's red high heels that I can barely walk in. Next, I put on tons of Mom's make-up. Her red lipstick is on my cheeks and my lips and her blue eye shadow is all over my face. Since Mom's hairspray is like spray-on glue, I tease my hair and spray the hairspray until my hair is sticking straight up. Yep, I look pretty crazy. Mom's dress is really long, so I have to hold it up while I walk down the stairs.

"Look at Joanna!" the second to the oldest hyena boy, Aaron, yells.

"Why do you look like a clown?" the third oldest, Byron, asks. The hyena boys are screaming and laughing so hard Mom comes running to the stairs.

"What on Earth?" Mom says.

"Excuse me, ma'am, I'm looking for Megan Roberts," I say in a British accent.

"And who are you?" Mom says.

"I am the royal queen of responsibilities who has to make her own decisions," I say in my best grownup queen voice.

"I see…well, I'll see if she's available to speak with you, your royal highness," Mom says. I wait at the stairs and try to ignore the hyena boys' high-pitched shrills. Megan's mouth almost hits the floor.

"What are you wearing?"

"I must speak with you in the formal bedroom at once," I say.

"Um, okay." She follows me up the stairs. In the formal bedroom area, I close and lock the door to keep the hyena boys out.

"Now, Megan dear, I am a queen with a lot of responsibilities, so I don't have much time on my schedule."

"Why are you talking like an old British lady?" Megan says, making me laugh.

"I am not an old British lady, Megan. I am the queen, so sit on the bed and stop interrupting, dear." Megan covers her giggles with her hands and sits on the bed.

"As I was saying before I was so rudely interrupted, I have many responsibilities and one of them is deciding if Riley can come over for a visit. I must remind you that during the days when I was Riley's friend, I was very unkind, and it seems I did not act like a very nice queen. In fact I didn't say anything at 'tall,'" I say in my accent. "You, being a very nice princess, were so kind to forgive me, and now your grace, I am hoping you can forgive my dear friend Riley who has been shunned by Tera, Queen of Bullyingham." I can see the teddy bear hamster in Megan's head running on the wheel.

"But how do you know we can trust Riley?" Megan asks.

"Excellent question, Princess Megan. I suppose we will just have to hope for the best," I say.

"And you can't go around telling everybody our personal business. Some things should stay personal."

"Agreed," I say.

"Okay, I'll give Riley a chance. You're crazy," Megan laughs.

"Please join me for dinner. We'll be having candy," I

announce. Mom keeps her promise and buys us tons of candy from the dollar store.

"I can't believe you got us candy for dinner!" Megan says. Wait until Megan finds out that if I save a cow from getting hit from a school bus, I can bring it home.

Saturday feels like my birthday even though it's not until July 21. Megan and I ate five cookies each at the church and we gave away twenty "need" bags, but I got an index card with a request we didn't have. When I asked Ms. Karyn what I should do about it she told me to hang onto it. Mom is on the phone with Riley's grandma and the only thing Mom is saying is, "Yes, I understand" and "Yes Ma'am," which I'm hoping means Riley can come over.

"What are you going to do about the need card?" Megan asks. I've been holding onto it ever since we left the church. For some reason, I can't stop thinking about it. The index card says:

Needs: (for my daughter, size "small," age 8)
Socks
School supplies
New clothes

We do have socks, but we don't give away clothes at the church, and there is no name on the index card.

"All right, nice talking to you as well, Ms. Johnson, bye-bye," Mom says.

"Is Riley coming?" I ask, jumping up and down.

"Yes she is. She'll be here in twenty minutes, so I want you to make sure all of your clothes are folded." Megan helps me fold my clothes and pick up my toys.

"What are we gonna do when Riley gets here?" she asks.

"I don't know yet, but I really need help with my star student poster. I don't know what I'm going to talk about. I don't play a sport, and I'm not in dance or theater. I don't really do anything." I set Emily on the bed.

"You help out at church on Saturdays," Megan says.

"I don't think that's something that I should put on a poster."

"Maybe other kids will want to help too," Megan says. The room is tidy and we have Apples to Apples and Uno ready in case Riley wants to play.

Megan and I go downstairs to greet Riley and her grandma. Riley is wearing jean shorts and a purple tank top. Her braids are in a ponytail. "Riley!" I give her a big hug. To my surprise, Megan gives her a hug too.

"I'll pick you up in a couple of hours," Riley's grandma says. I saved a few cookies from church for Riley, so I give her the cookies and we go upstairs to my room because it's the biggest next to Ms. Karyn's.

"Wanna play a game?" I ask.

"Sure," Riley says. Megan sets the cards up so we can play Apple to Apples.

"These cookies are good," Riley says.

"I told you, that's because they're homemade. Homemade beats store-bought every time," I say.

"We should help Joanna with her star student poster after this, because it's due on Monday," Megan says.

"It's supposed to be fun, but it feels like work," I admit.

"I'll help," Riley says. Megan and I look at each other. I know Megan is surprised to see Riley being so nice, but I'm not because I know Riley is not *that* much different from me.

Memory Verse 18

Philippians 4:4

"Always be filled with joy in the Lord. I will say it again. Be filled with joy."

My poster board is almost finished! Riley and Megan helped me take lots of pictures yesterday. Riley and her grandma were our guests at church this morning. Riley got to meet Ms. Bethany and Kiara, who was still a little mad that I didn't go to her birthday party. She forgot all about it though once I started taking pictures of her. Kiara loves to model for the camera. Mom is getting all of the pictures developed today. Tomorrow I'll be ready to present my star student poster. I know my entire class, including Mrs. Washington, will be so surprised.

"Where are we going?" I ask Mom as we pass the freeway that takes us to Ms. Karyn's house.

"You'll see," she says. Megan and I exchange confused looks while Ms. Stacy and Mom giggle. Mom turns into the mall parking lot and I grab Megan's hand.

"We're going to the mall?"

"Yup," Mom says. Megan squeezes my hand. I love going to the mall. Normally we only go just before school starts for back-to-school clothes, and I always get warm bite-sized cookies and tangy lime lemonade with a hot dog on a stick. I can already smell the cookies.

"Are we window-shopping today?" I ask, because a few times Mom and I have gone window-shopping to see what was new at the mall.

"Today, you girls are going on a little shopping spree," Mom says.

"A shopping spree?" I ask.

"So we're getting new clothes?" Megan asks.

"New clothes, new shoes, and you both have an appointment to get your nails painted."

"We're getting manicures!" I jump up and down.

"That's right," Mom laughs.

"Really?" Megan's eyes are as big as oranges. I can't believe we're going shopping for clothes and shoes and it's almost summer. Where did Mom and Ms. Stacy get so much money? Can we afford to do this? Mom pinches my cheek. I guess I let my thoughts draw mental pictures on my face.

"Ladybug, you need to lighten up. Go get yourself some new shoes and stop worrying so much," Mom says pointing towards the kids' shoe store.

"C'mon!" Megan pulls my hand. My heart does cartwheels inside my chest. The sandals I've wanted for a long time are right in front of me. I saw them when Mom and I went window-shopping a few months before she lost her job. They have a brown strap that connects to multicolor straps that look like braided bracelets, and they're wedges so they make me look taller.

"They're still here!" I hold the display sandal close to my acrobatic heart.

"Cool!" Mom smiles.

"Can I get them?" My hopes are already way high.

"Yes ma'am," Mom says. I like the sandals Megan's holding too; they look like someone made sandals out of jeans.

"Those are super cute, Megs," I say.

"I like yours too," Megan says. Mom pays for our sandals and we walk toward another shoe store.

"I think they need a pair for the park—what do you think, Ms. Stacy?" Mom says.

"Absolutely," Ms. Stacy says.

"Two pairs?" Megan and I say at the same time.

"Find what you like," Mom orders. Megan and I get matching purple, pink, and white sneakers.

"Let's pick out some outfits to go with your new shoes," Mom says. She and Ms. Stacy let us pick out our favorite outfits and a few accessories like bracelets and earrings. I find a best friend heart necklace that looks like it's broken into two pieces; one half says "Best" and the other half says, "Friends." Mom even lets us get the best friend necklace. The nail salon smells like cleaning day, when Mom and I clean our bathroom, but the foot massage feels awesome and it tickles too.

"This is the life," Megan sighs, laying her head on the big black leather chair.

"We should get pedicures every day," I say.

"If I had a million dollars, I would put a nail salon in my house," Megan says.

"I think they should put one at school so we can get

pedicures doing recess," I answer.

"No—they should put one in every classroom," Megan says. Mom and Ms. Stacy are reading magazines while Megan and I get our toes painted. I choose a purple glitter color and Megan chooses neon green.

"I have more clothes than I had before," Megan says.

"And underwear, now you have lots of underwear!" I yell. Megan laughs because Mom and Ms. Stacy heard me. My stomach full of bite-sized cookies and hot dog on a stick rumbles as I close my eyes and pretend to eat grapes and fan myself.

"Oh darling, I must have my driver bring me back here; this place is simply ravishing."

"Me too, darling." Megan plays along.

"I'll have my people call your people."

"No darling, your people are too busy building your new mansion. I'll have *my* people call *your* people."

"Oh no darling, my mansion can wait, your people are busy buying your private island, let *my* people call *your* people," I inflate my words like balloons.

"No, no, no darling, I insist," Megan shakes her head.

"Well then, I will fly your people on my private jet to my people at the mansion and they can discuss everything there."

"Yes darling, let's do that," Megan agrees.

Our nails and toenails dry and then we put on our new sandals.

"Did you have a good day, ladies?" Ms. Stacy asks.

"Yes! Thank you so much, Mommy," Megan says.

"Thanks, Mom," I say. Mom gives me a wink in the rearview mirror. I practice my presentation in my mind. At home, I put my poster and my star student notebook by my backpack.

"Are you excited?" Mom asks.

"And nervous. Nobody has ever done anything like this before."

"I love your idea. I think it's a great way of looking at things," Mom says. She helps me hang up all of my new dresses and jeans. I put away my new underwear and socks. The "need" card inside my drawer is staring at me. I pick it up and sit down on the bed.

"What's that?" Mom asks.

"It's an idea." I stare at the card. The idea came to me last night in a dream. In it, I saw kids walking to school like Mom did in the icy snow without a sweater or jacket. I had a big box full of sweaters and I yelled out, "Over here!" Then I passed out sweaters and jackets to all of the kids to keep them warm. When I woke up, I knew I wanted to give clothes to kids who needed them, but there was just one problem...where would I get the clothes?

I decide to ask Mom if she has any ideas. Turns out she has lots of good ideas and she's really excited to help.

"Oooh! I know!" Mom's eyes sparkle like firecrackers on the Fourth of July. "Quick, bring me the computer!" I run and grab the laptop Ms. Karyn lets us borrow. Mom points to the screen. There are a lot of organizations in Las Vegas that give away clothes to kids, she says. One organization says they will pick up the clothes from schools that have a "clothing drive."

"Do you think we can have a clothing drive at my school?" I ask.

"You can ask and find out," Mom says. So far, I've noticed most of the websites we've looked at only accept clothes that are "in season."

"That means since summer is coming up, you can ask for clothes that are appropriate for the summer, like short-sleeved shirts."

"And shorts," I add.

"Exactly. Why don't you grab my phone and find out more information so you can decide which organization you would like to work with and what their needs are. We want to make sure that the clothes that are donated will go directly to someone who needs them."

I make the phone calls and ask questions, and Mom writes down my answers. All of the organizations are really happy to help, and one will even donate flyers and posters. All I have to do now is get permission from my school and choose a week for the clothing drive. I really hope Mrs. Washington likes my idea and shares it with Mr. Suarez; I want other kids to have "back to school clothes" even though it's not really "back to school." Since our church doesn't give away clothes, maybe they can spread the word about our clothing drive. Megan, Ms. Karyn, and Ms. Stacy all think it's a great idea, but what will Mrs. Washington and Mr. Suarez think?

Memory Verse 19

Proverbs 18:24

"Some friends are fun to be with, but a true friend can be better than a brother."

My blood vessels are playing "double-Dutch" jump rope with my heart. Mrs. Washington kept my poster board hidden the entire day. Only Megan and Riley have seen it, because they helped me decorate it when Riley came over. I gave Mrs. Washington my star student journal this morning and she really liked it.

"My name is Joanna, I guess you already know," I say, standing in front of the class. "And this is me." The class is giggling and looking at each other, because my poster has been transformed into a cut-out of me. Mom had my school picture blown up to almost my size and Megan and Riley helped glue on pictures. I wipe my palms on my new jeans and take a deep breath.

"As you can see, this is our class picture." I point to the picture we took at the beginning of the school year.

"You're probably wondering why our class picture is glued to my forehead next to a hamster on a wheel," I laugh.

"Well, all of you are kids that I'll never forget, because this year has been a really hard year and many of you helped me remember that even though it's been hard I still have my friends." I look around the classroom. On my heart there are pictures of Ms. Karen, the hyena boys, Mr. Earl, and their house.

"This year, my mom lost her job and I had to move into their house. I think they are a part of me, because they helped us when we had no place to go. I hope that one day I'll be able to help them too," I say. I don't know what my classmates are thinking, but Megan is laying her head on her arms and she gives me a "thumbs up" sign so I think I'm doing okay.

"On my arms and legs are my friends and family." I show them a drawing of Mrs. Washington, and pictures of Kiara and Ms. Bethany. Mom, my cousins, and my aunts are on my legs and arms.

"They guide me and show me they love me, "I say, opening my arms. I point to the cross on my shoes.

"And God directs my steps." Now I really don't know what the class is thinking, because everyone is so quiet.

"This may not look like much, because it's just pictures of people, and it may not seem like I have a lot of stuff or I do a lot of cool things, but I think I have a lot because I have friends, family, and God and that's what matters to me. Thank you."

"Well done, Joanna." Mrs. Washington claps. My entire class cheers and some people whistle. I look at Riley and she's smiling at me. Mrs. Washington hangs my poster board in the front of the class next to the whiteboard; no poster has ever gone there before.

"Alright settle down, pack up, and get lined up at the door," Mrs. Washington says. As the star student I line up first. Lilia is right behind me.

"Great job," Lilia says.

"Thanks," I answer.

"My dad lost his job last year and it was hard too. We moved in with my cousins. We have our own apartment now, but for a while it was really cramped," she says.

"I bet you ate a lot of food."

"Yes! We had so much food!" She laughs.

"Us too," I say.

"Did your mom find a job yet?"

"Yeah, she did."

"That's good. I was gonna say my mom knows a lot of people and she could help her if she didn't find one yet. One of her friends helped my dad get his job," she says. I know Megan's mom is looking for a job, but I don't want to offer without Megan's permission.

"Thanks anyway."

"I'm sorry about the way I treated you on the field, Tera can be really mean. That's why we're not friends anymore," she says. I look down the line. Tera is at the end of the line. Mrs. Washington is walking towards the front of the line.

"I loved your presentation." Mrs. Washington smiles.

"Thanks," I say. On the blacktop I see Tera's mom yelling at a man next to the slide.

"What's going on there?" Mrs. Washington says, looking over at them. The man walks over to Mrs. Washington. Tera's mom looks really angry.

"I don't want my daughter going home with her! I have

full custody!" he shouts, waving a crumbled piece of paper.

"Tera is going home with me. I'm her mother!" Tera's mom shouts back.

"Please, allow me to dismiss the other children and then we can discuss this," Mrs. Washington says. Behind me, Tera is crying and my heart hurts for her. It's super embarrassing to have the entire school staring at you. Normally it's so loud after school I can't even hear myself think, but today everyone is staring at Tera's mom and dad. It's a gossip buffet.

"Let's go," Megan says. Her mom is taking us home today. Mr. Suarez is talking into his radio and jogging over to Tera's mom and dad.

"He's abusive! My daughter is not leaving with him!" Tera's mom cries.

"I'm abusive? You're crazy…" Tera's dad is saying a lot of bad words and now parents are scrambling to get their kids out of the gate. Mr. Suarez is standing between Tera's mom and dad.

"Let's calm down, please; there are children out here," Mr. Suarez says calmly. I run to catch up with Megan and Ms. Stacy and almost run into the gate trying to get a glimpse of Tera. I can still hear them yelling in the parking lot.

"No one should air their dirty laundry in public," says a parent walking by.

"Call the police!" another parent shouts. Mr. Felix, our school janitor, is asking parents to please leave so he can close the gate, but everyone is crowding around the gate watching. In the car, Ms. Stacy turns the radio on to drown out the noise.

"Poor Tera," I say to Megan. Megan is looking out the window. A police car is driving onto the school sidewalk!

"The police are here!" Megan points to the window.

"I hope Tera's okay," I say.

"Are you girls okay?" Ms. Stacy asks.

"Yes," Megan and I say together.

"I'm sorry you had to listen to all of that bad language and see that," Ms. Stacy says.

"My dad used to yell like that too," Megan whispers. I wonder if that's why Megan and her mom had to live in their car. Megan pulls my shirt so I lean towards her.

"He used to get really mad," Megan whispers.

"Is that why you lived in your car and in a motel?" I whisper back. Megan nods her head.

"We lived in a shelter because my dad used to hurt us, not a motel, but my mom told me not to tell," Megan whispers. I see Ms. Stacy looking at us in the rear-view mirror so I don't ask any questions. I'm so, so worried about Tera. Now that Lilia isn't friends with Tera anymore, Tera has no one to talk to.

"We have to talk to Tera tomorrow," I say. Megan's eyebrows look like they are attached to stings and someone pulled the strings all the way up.

"No, you can't. It's her personal business, Joanna. You can't just ask people's personal business all the time—Tera isn't even your friend anymore." Megan should know what it's like to wish you could talk to someone, but you feel like there's no one who would understand. I don't want Tera to feel like she has nobody to talk to and no friends. Even if she doesn't want to be my friend, she should at least know that I want to be her friend.

"Everybody saw what happened," I argue.

"Yeah, but maybe she doesn't want to talk about it. Just leave her alone."

"I just want her to know I'm her friend."

Megan rolls her eyes. "Tera doesn't want to be your friend or anybody else's. You're only going to make her more mad if you say something to her, and it's none of your business anyway," she says, making the number "8" with her neck as she talks.

I look out the window. I know Megan's right, it's "none of my business salad" staring me right in the face, but I can't help it. I feel something I can't explain, like an invisible force pushing me to talk to Tera. What if she yells at me for talking about her personal business? But what if she doesn't?

Mom looks tired, the way she did when she came home from her old job. "What did Mrs. Washington say about the clothing drive?" she asks, taking off her high-heeled work shoes. Her shoes are really smelly, like old garbage. I pinch my nose.

"My feet don't stink," Mom says.

"Mrs. Washington says I have to talk to the PTA about it." I breathe through my mouth.

"Okay, well they didn't say no, so that's a good sign. I'll find out how to get in touch with the PTA tomorrow and see what we can find out. How did your presentation go?"

"Good," I say. I would be happier, but I can't stop

thinking about Tera.

"Just good? What did Mrs. Washington say?" Mom asks.

"She said it was good."

"What did your class say?"

"Good," I answer.

"So everybody said 'good?'"

"Yeah," I sigh. Mom looks at me like she wants to say something else, but she takes off her earrings instead.

Memory Verse 20

John 10:27

"My sheep listen to my voice; I know them, and they follow me."

Megan, Riley, Lilia, and I are sitting at one table and Tera is sitting at the end of the table in front of us.

"Don't do it, Joanna," Megan warns. I want to invite Tera to sit with us at our table, but Megan, Riley, and Lilia don't want me to. I'm outnumbered.

"Just because I'm not mad at Tera anymore doesn't mean I have to be her friend," Megan adds.

"I don't even *want* to be her friend," Lilia says.

"I feel bad about what happened to her yesterday, but it's her own fault she has no one to sit with," Riley says. Tera is staring at her phone, and I notice she isn't eating her lunch.

"Maybe now that she has no friends she'll stop being so mean," Lilia says.

"Tera will never stop being mean," Riley says so loudly that Tera looks at us.

"Can we stop talking about Tera," I say.

"What do you want to talk about?" Lilia asks.

"I dunno, *not* Tera," I mumble.

"Oh my gosh, Tera just blocked me, look!" Riley says, showing Lilia her cell phone.

"She unfriended me too, like I care." Lilia rolls her eyes.

"Just ignore her," Megan says. Tera gets up from the table and walks into the bathroom, probably to get away from the noise.

"Why are you guys being so mean?" I say.

"I'm not being mean. Do you think I'm being mean?" Lilia asks.

Megan shakes her head. What happened to them? I get up from the table and follow Tera into the bathroom.

"Joanna!" I hear Megan yelling, but I don't turn around.

"Tera?" I call.

"Leave me alone," the muffled voice from behind the stall answers. I can hear the tears in her voice. I pinch my nose. Poor Mr. Felix, the girls' bathroom is so gross and kids don't care that he has to clean up their messes.

"I'm not leaving, so you might as well come out," I say.

"Go away!" Tera demands. Megan and the rest of the girls come into the bathroom.

"What are you doing in here?" Megan asks.

"None of your business," I say. Megan raises one eyebrow and giggles with Riley.

"Fine, stay in here." She stalks out of the bathroom.

"I don't know why you're chasing after her. She doesn't even like you," Lilia says. Tera opens the bathroom door because I'm quiet and she thinks we've all left. She moves past me and washes her hands. Her eyes and cheeks are cherry red.

"What do you want?" she says, drying off her hands.

"I just want you to know you can sit with us if you

124

want—or you can just sit with me," I say, because who would want to sit with them. I don't even want to sit with them anymore.

"Just leave me alone." Tera stalks out of the bathroom.

Megan looks different. I hardly recognize her with Lilia and Riley. They're doing everything Tera did that they hated. They're pointing at her and laughing and Tera is trying her best to pretend she doesn't notice. I'm not sitting with them. I'd rather sit by myself.

When the last bell rings, I don't walk with Megan on the blacktop and we don't talk on the way home. I do my homework by myself and Megan does her homework in her room. I never thought I would hate living with Megan, but now I can't wait till Mom and I move out. At dinner I'm invisible to her and she's invisible to me. Mom is working extra hours so we can move out faster and I'm glad. She must have forgotten all about the clothing drive, because she hasn't brought it up. I don't know if I even want to do it anymore because Megan and Riley were supposed to help me, but all they want to do is talk about Tera and make her feel bad.

The entire week is the same thing. I don't talk to Megan, Riley, or Lilia, they don't talk to me, Tera doesn't eat lunch, I barely see Mom, I do my homework, eat dinner, and go to bed. On Saturday, Mom and Ms. Stacy want to take Megan and me roller-skating, but we both say "no thanks." Megan's birthday is next week, so Mom wants me to help Ms. Stacy plan her party.

"What's going on between you two? " Mom asks while

we're picking out a gift for Megan.

"Megan's changed," I admit.

"How so?"

I don't want Megan to get in trouble for the way she's treating Tera. "I think we're growing apart," I say, remembering an episode of my favorite show when two best friends got into a really big fight and one girl said she was growing apart from the other girl.

"I see. Well, what are you gonna to do about it?" Mom asks.

Me? Why do I have to do anything about it? Every time I try to do something about things, it never works out.

"I don't know," I say, looking at a really cute pair of pajamas I know Megan would like.

"You're always full of ideas, I'm sure you can come up with something. By the way, I've been meaning to tell you, I talked to the PTA president and she wants to talk to you on Monday after school about the clothing drive."

"She does?" I thought Mom had forgotten about it.

"Yeah, she thinks it's a good idea for a fundraiser and she even has a contact with a local group that helps homeless youth and they will pay for the collected clothes," Mom says, taking the pajama pants off the rack. The hamster wakes up from her nap and starts running on my brain wheel.

"Perfect!" I hand Mom the matching pajama top. She's right—I do have an idea for the clothing drive.

"I'm glad you're excited about it," Mom says. I'm more than excited. This is the perfect opportunity. I find a doll that looks similar to Emily for Megan's birthday and hand it to Mom.

"Nice," she agrees. At home, I break the silence.

"Wanna jump rope outside?" I ask Megan. She peers out the window.

"It's getting hot," she says, turning back to the book she's reading on the couch.

"Maybe we can go swimming," I say.

"No thanks," she says without looking up from her book. There's only one way out of this.

"I'm sorry, Megan. I don't want to fight. You're my best friend," I plead.

"Then why did you stop talking to us?"

"You *know* why," I say, squinting my eyes.

"Yeah, because you wanted to be friends with Tera and then you got mad because nobody else did. Tera didn't even want to be your friend, but you couldn't let it go so you got mad at us," Megan says, sounding just like Lilia and Riley.

"I just want things to go back the way they were between us," I say. Megan nods, but she still looks different. Megan, Lilia, and Riley are the new group in our class that everyone wants to be a part of. They've become the circle of whisperers who point and laugh at any girl not in their circle. Even though they don't do it to me, they do it to other girls, especially Tera and Rachel, so it's just as bad. Megan knows what it feels like to be made fun of and so does Riley, so why are they doing this? I don't get it. They both complained about how mean Tera was to them, but they're doing the same thing they complained about.

If what I have to do means Megan and I can't be

friends then I guess we can't be friends, which really makes me sad. I thought Megan knew what it was like to be on the outside, but maybe she never really did. Maybe it's just me and most kids don't hate going to school the way I did. Maybe no one, not even Megan, knows what it's like to find a note that is so mean the only safe place is a disgusting bathroom. Maybe no one has ever wished they were invisible the way I have. Maybe I'm the only kid at Elaine Bavak Elementary School who is sick and tired of the circle of whisperers, the pointing, and the "you can't sit with us," or "don't sit with them." There are too many kids at my school to count, but I wonder how many of them feel the same way. There's only one way to find out.

Memory Verse 21

Philippians 4:13

"Christ is the one who gives me the strength I need to do whatever I must do."

Ms. Mariana is the PTA president at our school. She's meeting me in the cafeteria after school. Ms. Stacy and Megan are waiting for me at another table. Megan is doing her homework and Ms. Stacy is reading Mom's job interview book from the library. Ms. Mariana is a little taller than me. She looks the same age as Mom, with curly brown hair that barely reaches her chin, and she's wearing a brown dress. I'm a friend of her son, Emilio, who used to go to Safe Zone last year.

"I'm so glad to hear that you want to start a clothing drive for our school. The non-profit we work with said they have a need for sweaters and coats," she says.

"But it's almost summer," I say.

"Yes, but they want to start preparing for winter, when they don't get as many donations because many parents are buying sweaters and coats for their own children."

"Oh. That makes sense," I say. "I have an idea for the clothing drive."

"What's your idea?" Ms. Mariana scratches her head with her long nails while resting her elbow on the table.

"Kids can say "no" to bullying by donating clothes."

Ms. Mariana tilts her head to the side. I can tell she is thinking by the way she's looking up at the ceiling, her eyes moving from left to right.

"We've never tied an anti-bullying campaign to a clothing drive before. I'd have to speak to the organization and Mr. Suarez about that."

"Okay." I nod.

"We do have the book fair coming up next week. Maybe we could do it during that week." That would be awesome—so many kids and parents go to the book fair.

"Yeah, and we can say that anyone who is being bullied and wants the bullying at our school to stop can donate an item of clothing."

"Hmmm...I don't know about that. I don't believe everyone would agree there's an issue with bullying at our school. As you know, we have a zero tolerance for bullying and Mr. Suarez is VERY committed to addressing every incident. If someone is being bullied or they witness any form of bullying, all they have to do is report it and it will be immediately addressed. I think everyone is aware of that, and to say that would be assuming there is an issue."

Yeah, I think, but what about the stuff that happens that he doesn't know about? It took a long time for me to tell Mrs. Washington that Tera made fun of me pretty much the whole school year, because I was too afraid to tell anyone. Maybe Mr. Suarez will see that there *is* still a problem at our school even though we have a "no bullying" policy when he sees how many sweaters and coats are being donated.

"I think we should do the clothing drive and leave it at that. It's worked really well for us in the past, and I don't want it to become something that it's not meant to be," Ms. Mariana says.

"But maybe there's a lot of things that Mr. Suarez doesn't know about, and if a lot of kids donate a sweater then maybe he will know that it's still a problem," I say.

"I'll talk to him about it, but I can tell you right now it's highly unlikely that it's going to happen. Kids know they can speak up, and it doesn't have to be a teacher. They can talk to the school nurse, or tell their parents, or even a friend who can report it for them. I don't think it's necessary to merge the two together. I think our school has bullying pretty well handled."

"What if kids are too scared or embarrassed to tell someone?" I ask. Ms. Mariana takes a deep breath and blinks really fast.

"Like I said, I don't think that would work, and even if we did do it, kids might not want to ask their parents to donate if it's tied to bullying. The goal is to raise money for the school, but we won't do that if children are too intimidated to ask their parents to donate," she says.

"But let me talk to Mr. Suarez and the organization and I'll get back to you about it okay?" She stands up.

"Okay, thank you."

"You're welcome," she says. I walk to Ms. Stacy.

"So, how did it go?" Megan asks. I didn't tell her about my idea for the bullying part, just that I wanted to start a clothing drive.

"Fine, "I say.

"Cool. I think it will help a lot of kids. I know it would have helped me," she says. I'm thinking about what Ms. Mariana said about kids being too embarrassed to ask their parents if it's about bullying. Would I have asked my mom at the beginning of the year?

I guess I can see Ms. Mariana's point that maybe kids won't donate anything at all because they won't want to talk about it with their parents, but I don't see why we can't try it. Even if only one kid donates a sweater or a coat doesn't that mean there's a problem? Mr. Suarez said at our assembly that "every kid matters." Ms. Mariana wants to raise a lot of money for the school and one sweater won't raise a lot of money, but it might help someone not be so afraid. Doesn't that matter too?

I tell Mom while I'm doing my homework upstairs and she agrees with me. "I think it's a wonderful idea, and hopefully Mr. Suarez will see it that way too."

"But Ms. Mariana didn't think so," I confess.

"Well that doesn't mean it's not a good idea; she just sees things from a different perspective. People are entitled to their own opinions just like you are entitled to yours. And she didn't say you couldn't have a clothing drive right?"

"Right," I agree.

"So let's focus on the positives, and not worry so much about the other stuff, okay? Either way it's a good thing and it's about helping kids," Mom says. The doorbell rings. Ms. Karen, Ms. Stacy, and Megan are downstairs. I hear laughter and voices.

"Who's here?" I ask. When I open the door, I see Riley running with Megan into her room. Megan didn't even tell me that Riley was coming over!

"Hey Riley," I say, sticking my head out the door.

"Hey," she says. Megan closes the bedroom door.

"Riley's here," I pout.

"That's nice, why don't you go say hi," Mom says.

"I did," I say, biting my bottom lip.

"Oh, okay." Mom picks up her cell phone. She's talking to my Aunt Nisha now about her new job, so she doesn't notice my lips are trembling. I live here too and they might have their little circle at school, but Megan is not going to do it here. I march across the hallway and bang on the door. Riley is dancing to music coming from her cellphone.

"Yeah?" Megan holds the door like she's the gatekeeper.

"What are you guys doing?"

"Dancing!" Riley yells. Megan holds back a giggle.

"Can I come in?" I ask. Megan looks back at Riley like she needs her permission.

"Um…we're kind of in the middle of something," Megan says.

"Oh, okay," I say.

"Sorry," Megan says slowly closing the door. I can hear Megan and Riley laughing and I even hear Megan pretending to be me saying, *"Can I come in?",* but in this whiny baby voice. I don't sound like that. My voice is very mature. I bang on the door again.

"Yes?" Megan says, pushing hair out of her face.

133

"So why are you making fun of me? I can hear you, you know."

Riley comes to the door. "No one is making fun of you—just let her come in," she mumbles. Megan opens the door wide then walks towards her bed.

"Let's call Lilia," Riley says.

"Yeah!" Megan agrees. They huddle on the bed like two best friends while I'm standing beside them. Lilia answers the Facetime call.

"Oh my gosh, did you see how Rachel was acting around Jake? You know she likes him," Lilia says. Megan and Riley both laugh. I guess I'm invisible.

"You guys wanna play Apples to Apples?" I ask.

"That game is for little kids," Riley says. Megan doesn't say anything, but I guess Megan's a little kid too, because she used to love to play with me and now that Riley's here with her fancy smartphone, she thinks it's babyish. I guess she's going to hate what I got her for her birthday, because she probably thinks dolls are for little kids now too.

"Did you see what Tera posted about 'fake friends?'" Riley asks. I wonder if Megan knows that the only reason Riley has a cell phone is so that her grandma can reach her for emergencies. I heard her grandma tell Mom one night when Mom put her on speakerphone she's not even allowed to be any social media websites. Megan is acting like she doesn't even see me, so I leave and help Ms. Karen set the table downstairs.

"Hey, Ms. Joanna," Ms. Karen says.

"Hi," I say with a big smile.

"Why aren't you upstairs with the girls?" she asks.

"I'd rather be down here," I say. Ms. Karen nods.

"Well since you're down here, would you like to help the boys and me get ready for dinner?" she asks.

"Sure," I say. Anything is better than being ignored.

Memory Verse 22

The best friend necklace is still around my neck, but Megan isn't wearing hers. Mom doesn't have to go to work today because Mr. Suarez called her this morning; he wants to talk to us in his office about the clothing drive. I hope it's good news, but since Ms. Mariana didn't like my idea about bullying maybe it won't be *all* good news.

"Don't bite your nails." Mom pushes my hand away from my mouth as we walk on the blacktop. Megan runs to meet Lilia and Riley while Mom and I head toward the office. Our class is lining up with Mr. Nguyen's class. Mrs. Washington must be absent today.

"Do you think it's something bad?" I ask.

"Remember what I told you yesterday? Focus on why you want to do the clothing drive," Mom says.

The office lady with the red hair tells us to have a seat until Mr. Suarez comes to get us. I bite my nails again and Mom gives me "the look," so I peel off one last nail and chew on that.

"Thanks for coming in." Mr. Suarez shakes Mom's hand. We follow him down the hallway into his office, where Mrs. Washington is sitting. She isn't smiling, and her eyes look smaller than normal, like something heavy is weighing her eyelids down. Mr. Suarez closes the door and now I know for sure it's bad news.

"I wanted to talk to you because Mrs. Washington and I are concerned about Joanna's feelings regarding bullying at this school. As you know, we take bullying very seriously at this school and we never want a student to feel afraid to let us know when something is going on," Mr. Suarez says. He's wearing a tie with yellow smiley faces on it, but he's not smiling.

"Joanna, you know you can always tell me if there's something going on in the classroom," Mrs. Washington says.

Mom covers her teeth with her tongue and makes a smacking noise when her tongue lets go. She blows out air and turns her eyebrows into a pile of wrinkles.

"Well, I appreciate your concern. This is about the meeting Joanna had with Mariana yesterday after school, correct?" Mom says in a stern voice. I bite my pinky fingernail; it's the only one that still has a nail long enough to bite.

"Well, yes, I spoke with her," Mr. Suarez starts.

"Okay, well Joanna *has* spoken to me about it and her desire to give a voice to students who may not feel comfortable speaking up is about helping other students. You know what? I don't think this is a conversation that Joanna needs to participate in or miss class for, so I'm going to send Joanna back to class and we can discuss this amongst ourselves," Mom says, turning toward me. I stand up, give

Mom a kiss, and head to class. Walking slowly, I can hear Mom talking louder and faster.

"If there *were* an issue at my school, I can assure you it would be addressed. Please allow me to finish," Mr. Suarez says, talking over Mom as the door closes. I blow out a sigh. I didn't mean for all this to happen, I just wanted to help kids and now it's turning into this whole big "thing." I go to our classroom, but no one's in the class. I forgot our class is in Mr. Nguyen's class. Mr. Nguyen's class is only a couple of classrooms away, but I want to go to the bathroom before I have to see Megan, Riley, and Lilia. The bathroom is perfect and empty. No angry people or circle of whisperers.

How do I tell Mom that I don't want to do the clothing drive anymore? How do I tell Mrs. Washington that our class isn't what she thinks it is? How do I tell other kids to speak up if I can't even speak up? Everything feels murky like swamp water, except there's quicksand at the bottom and I'm slowly sinking. The recess bell rings. I better go to class before Mrs. Washington comes back.

Leaving the bathroom, I see Mrs. Washington walking down the hallway. Should I wait for her or pretend I don't see her? I wait because she's already seen me.

"I'm sorry about what happened," I say.

"No, no, no," Mrs. Washington shakes her head. "There's nothing for you to be sorry about," she says in a half-whisper.

"Mrs. Washington, there's a lot of things that you don't know about," I say. If I want other kids to be brave, I have to be brave first.

"Let's talk in the classroom," Mrs. Washington says. We walk into our classroom. It feels weird being the only ones in class. Mrs. Washington turns the blue chair around and sits at Evan's desk. *Be brave, Joanna.*

"I wasn't trying to get you in trouble," I say. Mrs. Washington's eyes brighten.

"You didn't get me in trouble," she says, looking the way Mom does when a sad puppy commercial comes on TV.

"I got my idea because a lot of girls in our class make fun of other girls. At lunch and at recess they whisper to each other, they laugh and point at each other. I know it doesn't seem like that's bad, but it feels bad when someone is doing it to you. I used to hate coming to school because of it. I think there might be other kids who hate coming to school too because they don't want to get made fun of or they don't want to be the only person who didn't get an invitation to a party, or they don't want people making fun of the way they look. I didn't tell you because some of those girls used to be my friends and one of them used to be my best friend. If a lot of kids donated sweaters or coats then maybe Mr. Suarez would see that a lot of kids are afraid to speak up about it."

"And what do you think he should do about it—let me rephrase that, what do you think would be a good solution?" Mrs. Washington is always trying to get us to find solutions to our problems in class.

"I think if a lot of kids say, 'I'm not going to be a part of it' or 'I'm going to speak up if I see it,' then that would help. Like, if everyone in our class brought a sweater and said, 'I'm not going to make fun of anyone,' then no one would make fun of anyone. That's all I was trying to do, but I didn't mean to make it this whole big thing. Maybe it was a stupid idea." I can't believe tear water is flooding my eyes in front of Mrs. Washington.

"I understand exactly what you're saying, and I'm so grateful that you shared it with me," Mrs. Washington says. Her eyes are teary too and I can feel she really means it.

"I know how scary it is to speak up because you don't want anyone to retaliate against you, or you might feel embarrassed that it's happening. It's tough and I totally understand, because it happened to me when I was in school and no matter how many rules might be in place, people find sneaky little ways around them. Listen to me, I promise I will do everything in my power to help you with your idea because it *is* a problem at our school and a lot of schools. It's not just our class and it's not just you, and you're right that something needs to be done about it. We don't have to just accept it or pretend like it doesn't exist. We're going to do this—together." She holds up her hand for a high-five. I give her a high-five and then a hug because she makes me smile. I don't know why I was so scared to tell her before. Maybe it's because she's nice, but can also be strict, like Mom.

"Let me show you something." She stands up. We walk to her desk and she pulls out her cell phone. She scrolls through pictures of her two Chihuahuas, Tom and Jerry, and then she stops at a picture of a quote with flowers around the quotation marks.

"This is one of my favorite quotes. It says, 'be a person

who makes another person look forward to tomorrow.' I love this quote because it helps us remember that everyone matters, and how you treat people matters."

"I like that quote too," I say. Mrs. Washington and I find Mr. Nguyen on the blacktop. Mrs. Washington is watching Megan, Riley, and Lilia closely.

Lunchtime is the same, except Mrs. Washington is still watching…everything. Rachel is sitting by herself and Tera didn't come to school today.

"Hey," I say, sitting down next to Rachel.

"Hi." Rachel opens her chocolate milk.

"I brought cookies, want one?"

"Sure." She smiles.

No one can turn down cookies, especially Ms. Jessica's cookies.

I'm happy to see that Mom is picking me up after school. She's wearing jeans, her silky pink tank top, and flat pink shoes that look like ballerina slippers; her hair is in twists, and she doesn't look mad.

"How was school, ladybug?" she asks.

"It was awesome. Mrs. Washington says she wants to help with my clothing drive."

"She did?" She glances at Mrs. Washington.

"Yeah, and she likes my idea."

"Well, I don't want you to be disappointed if Mr. Suarez disagrees, because it seems he's already made his decision about it."

"But Mrs. Washington said—"

"I understand, but Mr. Suarez has the final say and that's not what he wants to do, so we have to respect his decision and keep it moving, right?"

"Yes ma'am," I say, even though Mom didn't let me finish telling her that Mrs. Washington promised to do everything she could to help. Since Ms. Stacy picked up Megan from school early to take her to a dentist appointment, it's just Mom and me again.

"I was thinking we could get some frozen yogurt," Mom says.

"With hot fudge and sprinkles?"

"Of course, that's the only way to eat it." It's nice being at Ms. Karen's house with so many people and yummy food, but it's nice being with just Mom too.

Memory Verse 23

Ecclesiastes 4:9

"Two people are better than one. When two people work together, they get more work done."

Mrs. Washington called Mom early this morning and asked if she could talk to me in the classroom before school. The sun is just waking up, stretching into the clouds and yawning its rays over the mountains. I nibble Ms. Karen's blueberry muffins while Mom finds a parking spot along the sidewalk.

"Do you want me to walk you?" Mom picks up her coffee from the drink holder.

"Nope," I say, leaning over to give her a kiss.

"Alright, have a good day, sweetheart."

The office lady with the red hair buzzes me in and I walk down the long hallway past the pictures of the teachers hanging on the wall, the bathrooms, and the computers to my classroom. Mrs. Washington is sitting at her desk writing something.

"Good morning," she says.

"Good morning." Mrs. Washington has two blue folders and two pencils; she gives one folder and pencil to me.

"First, take out your agenda, it's the first page. You'll see I've scheduled a special meeting with all of the teachers and Mr. Suarez on Thursday at 7:30 so you can present your ideas and how you think the clothing drive will help prevent bullying at our school. I've already talked to your Mom and she's agreed to let you come. You'll notice the second page in your folder is an outline for your presentation. You'll need to come up with good arguments to support your claims. Also, I've got poster boards at my desk and you're more than welcome to work on them during free time in class or before school around this time."

"What are the poster boards for?" I take the other papers out of the folder.

"You'll want to make a few signs for the clothing drive, find a catchy title, show them what your goals are, and how you plan to advertise your clothing drive. I've included a few tips on how to do that in your folder. Let me know if you need help with anything," Mrs. Washington says.

"Can I start working on the posters now?"

"Sure, grab whatever you need." I pick out a hot pink poster board and a white one. Mrs. Washington has puffy paint, glitter, ribbons, glue sticks, markers, pretty much anything you can think of to make an awesome poster. I pull out the paper inside the folder about making a slogan. The first tip is to keep it simple. Hmm…the next tip says "stick to the point."

"Mrs. Washington? What do you think about, 'don't be a bully goat, donate a coat?'" Mrs. Washington squints like the sun is in her eyes.

"I don't like the goat part," she says. I'm back to the drawing board.

"Remember, first you need to make your message clear, but you can't do that unless you know what the message is. Is it 'Say no to bullying by donating a sweater or a coat'?"

"I want every kid who is being bullied to donate a sweater or a coat," I say.

"Well, I think we already know that bullying is still a problem, so this isn't about proving it's going on, it's about prevention and finding solutions."

"Okay, yeah, what if it's like the Presidential campaign and the message is 'vote no on bullying'?" I remember seeing bumper stickers that said "Vote No" with a check mark.

"I like that, that's a good one," she nods.

"How about 'Cast your vote and donate a coat'," I say.

"Perfect!" Mrs. Washington gives me a "thumbs up" sign. I draw a blue check mark and write the words.

"Can I print out a picture of a coat?"

"You can do whatever you want to decorate it," Mrs. Washington says. She lets me print out all the pictures I want and she doesn't even get mad that I'm printing so much stuff. I make four posters for coats and four sweater posters; two of the sweater posters say "Make a life better, donate a sweater," and the other two say "Make YOUR life better, donate a sweater." I decorate the pictures of sweaters with puffy paint, glitter, and ribbons.

"Mrs. Washington? Can some of the teachers help me with a part of my presentation? They don't need to bring anything, but they have to meet with me before the presentation so I can show them what to do."

"I'll send them an email and ask," she says, hanging up

the posters to dry. Ideas are flying around me like paper airplanes landing in my brain.

"We've gotta go." Mrs. Washington glances at the clock on the wall. I'm done with my posters. All I have to do now is write my presentation and the special part for the teachers. Mrs. Washington puts on her sunglasses, and we walk outside to the blacktop. The bell hasn't rung yet, so the circle of whisperers is on the playground. Tera is standing alone on the blacktop with a row of backpacks where our class lines up.

"Good morning, Ms. Tera," Mrs. Washington says.

"Good morning." Tera looks up.

"Hi Tera," I say.

"Hi," she says back.

"I like your shirt." Her shirt has a robin standing on a tree branch on the front.

"Thanks," she says, looking down at it. The bell rings and the kids in our class run to get the backpacks that saved their places in line.

"No talking, girls, make a straight line please." Mrs. Washington points to Megan, Riley, and Lilia sticking out of the line. I look down the line for Rachel. She's behind them, which isn't the safest place to be. In class, everyone is pointing and whispering about my posters, but even when kids ask, Mrs. Washington doesn't tell anyone why they're there.

I look forward to lunch all morning because I like sitting with Rachel. Tera is sitting by herself, and Kylie, the quietest girl in my class, is the newest member of the circle of whisperers.

"Let's sit over here," I say, holding my lunch tray. We're having sweaty hot dogs again. Mom was too tired this morning to make my lunch. I sit next to Tera.

"Hey Tera," I say.

"Hi," she says, staring at her phone.

"Hi," Rachel says. Tera gives a little wave.

"Whatcha' looking at?" I ask Tera.

"It's a game." She turns the screen towards me.

"How do you play?"

"You have to try to move the ball into the same color as the ball without touching any other colors in the obstacles."

"Can I try?" Tera hands me her phone. My turn is over on the first obstacle and Tera laughs.

I laugh too. "This game is hard,"

"You have to practice," she says.

"Can I try?" Rachel asks. Tera gives her phone to Rachel and she only makes it to the first round too. We're taking turns playing the game until lunch is over. I can see Megan staring at me out of the corner of my eye, but when I look at her she looks away.

"So you're friends with Tera again?" Megan asks after school as Ms. Stacy turns the radio on in the car.

"Yeah," I say.

"I thought you didn't like her."

"I never said that."

"Why did you go to school early today?" Megan asks.

"I'm working on something with Mrs. Washington."

"What are you working on?"

"The clothing drive."

"I hope you're not inviting Tera to my birthday party, because she's not invited." Megan crosses her arms.

"I don't wanna to talk about Tera." I look out the window. Megan looks out the other window. We ride to Ms. Karyn's house without saying another word.

I do my homework upstairs because I don't want to argue with Megan at the table. Even though we live together, we hardly see each other because Megan stays in her room or she goes outside and plays with other whisperers in the neighborhood who only eat juicy gossip steaks for lunch. So I stay indoors and help Ms. Karyn with dinner or dishes.

I tear out a piece of paper and make brainstorm bubbles for my presentation ideas. One of the tips from the folder Mrs. Washington gave me says "Speak from your heart." I write down everything that's in my heart into the bubbles and scribble out the ones I don't want to say. Mrs. Washington says I should paint a picture with my words. I have to make sure my audience sees the whole picture and not just a piece of it; otherwise they may see an entirely different picture. The picture I am painting with my words is a mask with many different colors. I want my audience to peel away the mask so they will see what's really behind the words.

Memory Verse 24

Psalm 118:24
"This is the day the Lord has made.
Let us rejoice and be happy today!"

No one has read my presentation speech, not even Mom or Mrs. Washington. Mrs. Washington and I set up the posters I made around the cafeteria. Mom is here, because her new boss said she could go to work later so she could stay and watch my presentation. Mr. Suarez walks in with more teachers. Now the jumping jellybeans in my stomach are making me feel nauseous.

"I'm nervous," I mumble to Mrs. Washington as she fixes the blue ribbon in my hair. We're standing beside the stage. There are so many teachers here, and Ms. Mariana is here too.

"Don't be nervous, you're going to do great," she says.

"I can't help it, what if I mess up?"

"All you have to do is use your imagination and pretend that everyone out there has a paintbrush and they have to paint whatever you tell them to paint with your words. Think about what picture you want them to see, and why it's so very important that they see it. They're all here to learn from you; you're their teacher."

"But what if they don't like the picture that they see?"

"Art speaks to us all in different way, but the artist

brings it to life. What matters is that you have brought us all together for a good cause, and that's pretty cool." Mrs. Washington smiles. I smile too. I'm an artist, so I hold up my canvas that is my speech and walk onto the stage with my head high. Mr. Suarez runs up and lowers the microphone because it's too high for me.

"Thank you all for coming," I say. Some of the teachers are looking at their cell phones.

"Let's begin." Four teachers that I asked to help me with my presentation come on stage, because "Let's begin" is their cue. Three of the teachers stand in a whisper circle on the stage and one teacher stands a few feet away. One of three teachers in the whisper circle begins to laugh and the other teachers look at Ms. Taylor standing by herself. I can see the teachers in the audience are now watching closely. They are doing a great job of showing what a whisper circle looks like. It's my turn now.

"Ms. Taylor? How did you feel when the teachers in the whisper circle were laughing at you and pointing at you?" Ms. Taylor takes the microphone.

"I'm the new kid on the block; this is my first year teaching and I know what it feels like to feel outside of the circle. It doesn't feel good at all," Ms. Taylor says.

"Thank you," I say. The teachers join the audience. It's time to paint my word picture.

"Mr. Suarez has done a great job with showing students how they can report bullying. I know that a circle of whisperers doesn't seem like that big of a deal, but it is for me and I think for a lot of kids. I think even though a lot of kids know they can tell a teacher or Mr. Suarez if they are being bullied at school, a lot of kids are still really scared to speak up. I know because I was one of them. All year a girl in my class would make fun of me and laugh at me. I wanted to be her friend so that she would stop, but then she started doing it to other people, and I told Mrs. Washington and Mr. Suarez. Later on, I found a note in my desk with no name on it that said, "Why is Joanna so ugly?" Even though there are rules in place to stop bullying, kids know they can still leave other kids out, and do things so they won't get in trouble because they know a lot of kids will be too scared to tell on them."

"I want to do two things," I say. "First, I want to make kids feel better about speaking up if someone is bullying them or if they see someone else being bullied. Second, I want to make it hard for kids to bully other kids because they know that someone will speak up. I think we can do both with the clothing drive and help kids in our local community who need sweaters and coats. As you can see, I have a lot of ideas for posters for our new anti-bullying campaign, like 'speak up and vote "NO" on bullying.' Also, 'Make a life better, donate a sweater,' and my personal favorite, 'cast your vote and donate a coat.' Every time a kid brings in a coat or a sweater, they will be casting their vote to let the bullies know we will not suffer in silence. I think with the clothing drive and the anti-bullying campaign we can change our school and make every kid know their voice matters. If you would like to help me change our school one coat and sweater at a time, please vote 'yes' to my idea.

Thank you."

The entire cafeteria full of teachers stands up and claps for me. Even Ms. Mariana claps for me. Mr. Suarez is looking around the room and watching. Mrs. Washington joins me on stage and I give her the microphone.

"Well done, Joanna. I just want you all to know that Joanna is not alone. I believe in what she's saying and I think creating an anti-bullying atmosphere at our school needs to be a top priority. Mr. Suarez does an excellent job at making the consequences for bullying tough, and while I think our bullying policies are effective as far as consequences are concerned, we do need to do a better job at educating our students about what bullying looks like by explaining the many different types of bullying so they understand that emotional intimidation is just as much a form of bullying as physical or verbal bullying. This is something that I firmly believe needs to be addressed, because disciplinary statements often paint an incomplete picture of our students," she says.

"I agree," one teacher says. Many other teachers nod. Mr. Suarez walks onto the stage and Mrs. Washington hands him the microphone.

"Joanna did an outstanding job," he says. The teachers clap again. "I *would* like to add that it is equally important that our faculty is well-educated in all aspects of bullying and I will be implementing a professional development training to support student engagement, because it can be difficult to identify and assess the types of bullying that aren't easily identified without the necessary training. We've done a great job at providing the best possible environment for our students, but we're always growing and the social climate of the school is always changing. I want to thank all of you for taking the time to be here and I also want to thank Joanna for having the courage to speak up. This is something that I think will be good for our school, and one thing I would like to make clear is that we are always willing to do more when are students are concerned and our efforts will be continuous. Thank you everyone," Mr. Suarez says.

Mom runs over to me as the teachers are leaving the cafeteria. "You did so well! I'm so proud of you!" She squeezes me hard.

"Mom—I can't breathe."

"My little ladybug!" She beams and kisses my cheeks. Mr. Suarez comes over to us with Mrs. Washington and shakes Mom's hand.

"I've got members of my staff working on this, and we'll start the campaign with the book fair next week. The nonprofit organization that we work with loves the idea, and we're looking forward to great things," Mr. Suarez says.

"Awesome!" I jump up and down.

"She did a wonderful job," Mr. Suarez says to Mom. Mom is smiling so big I bet her cheeks hurt.

"Well, I've got to get going, but great job, Joanna," Mr. Suarez says.

Now that the clothing drive and the anti-bullying campaign have a green light, Mrs. Washington says we still have a lot of work to do. I'm going to be the coordinator, so I have to work with Ms. Mariana and the organization to create the parent letters and educational materials for the classroom. Mrs. Washington also wants me to help with making more posters to go around the school. I'm also going to be the president of the new "Vote 'No' to bullying" committee that is made up of students. Every month we will have a special meeting to discuss new ideas for our anti-bullying campaign. Mr. Suarez will review them.

In class, Mrs. Washington gives me time before the bell rings to talk about what we're doing. Everyone raises their hands to help, including Megan, Lilia, and Riley.

"Can I help you sort the sweaters?" Megan asks.

"Sure, we'll be the sweater girls," I say "I need all the help I can get. I hope we get a lot of donations so that this winter will be a warm winter for a lot of kids."

"I think what you're doing is really cool," Megan says after school.

"Thanks for helping," I say.

At home, Ms. Karen wants to know if I can talk to Ms. Jessica about starting a clothing drive at our church. "Sure," I say. She doesn't know it, but I keep the "need" card in my pocket and I carry it with me everywhere I go. Mom and Ms. Stacy are getting T-shirts made for the volunteers who want to help. I hope kids aren't scared to talk to their parents, but I guess I won't know until Monday.

Memory Verse 25

1 Chronicles 16:11
Depend on the Lord for strength.
Always go to him for help.

The parent letters went out on Friday and so did the invitations to Megan's birthday party this weekend. Ms. Karyn and Mr. Earl have turned their gigantic back yard into such a cool place that I barely recognize it, and the hyena boys are at their grandparents' house for the whole weekend. There are four long tables under the gazebo. Each table is a different station. There's a drink station with blue Hawaiian punch "pool water" and colorful cups. Another table has green and blue beach pails with yellow shovels to scoop out chips, popcorn, and goldfish. My favorite table is the candy table. It looks so yummy, but I'm not allowed to eat any of it until the party starts. Some of the things on the candy table are Lifesaver gummy candies in a silver little bucket with a sign that says, "Grab a Floatie" and a jar with sour yellow, red, and blue licorice labeled "Pool Noodles."

Mr. Earl is barbecuing hamburgers and hot dogs on the grill. They smell so good I'm floating on the aroma. There's a game station too, with water balloons, squirt guns, and a bubble machine. Megan's beach ball cake is pretty awesome; it's strawberry and buttercream, and the cupcakes around the beach ball are a mixture of chocolate and vanilla. Megan is wearing a blue and white striped bikini, and I'm wearing the same one-piece bathing suit I wore to Tera's swim party. Mr. Earl made this really awesome beach ball party arch in the front yard and a surfboard sign that says "Come on around back for Megan's 10th birthday party." Kiara, our friend from church, just got here, and Riley's on her way. I'm helping Ms. Karen fold the towels and put them into the coolers while Megan helps Mom with the sunglasses and sunscreen station.

"I'm so hungry," I say, breathing in the hamburger air.

"Go tell Mr. Earl to make you a burger," Ms. Karyn says, but Mom shakes her head.

"She can wait and eat with everyone else," Mom says, making my stomach grumpy. It's growling at Mom, but she can't hear because the bubble machine is so loud. My stomach is used to eating a big breakfast, so I get hungry faster than I used to. Ms. Karyn hands me a granola bar, but I'd rather be hungry because it's one of her healthy bars and it tastes nasty.

"No thank you," I say.

"You see? If she were hungry she wouldn't be so picky," Mom says. Lilia is here too and she's wearing a one-piece like me.

"Hi Joanna!" She waves.

"Hey," I wave back.

"I think we're done here," Ms. Karyn says as Riley opens the sliding glass doors.

"Riley!" Megan shrieks, doing a dance.

"Joanna, come dance with us," Megan says. Kiara is

dipping her feet in the pool by herself so I decide to sit with Kiara instead.

"I don't know anybody except for you and Megan," Kiara says.

"Most of the kids coming are from our school," I say.

"When can we eat?" Kiara asks.

"I was thinking the same thing. I'll ask if we can start eating." I get up. Ms. Stacy is in the house talking to parents and putting Megan's presents away.

"A lot of people are getting hungry, Mom," I say as I pass her.

"Who's a lot of people? You?" Mom laughs.

"Kiara's hungry too. Can I ask Ms. Stacy if we can start eating, please?"

"Sure Joanna." In the house, Ms. Stacy is opening the door for Tera and her mom.

"Welcome," Ms. Stacy says.

"Hi," Tera's mom says. I really didn't think Tera would come, but I'm glad she's here. Tera's mom is looking at me. I think she remembers me. "Is your mom here?" she asks.

"*My* mom?" I point to myself.

"Yes," she says.

"Yeah, she's outside. I'll go get here," I run to the sliding glass door.

"Tera's (breath) mom (breath) is (breath) here, and she wants to talk to you," I struggle.

"Oh, okay," Mom says, scrunching her eyebrows. I don't know why I'm scared, but I hope Tera's mom doesn't yell at Mom. I follow closely behind her into the house. Mr.

Earl is setting up the speaker to play music outside.

"Hi, I'm Gwyneth, Tera's mom. Is there someplace we can talk?"

"Sure," Mom says, loosening her eyebrows. I wanna come too; I wanna know what Tera's mom wants to say to Mom, but I can tell by the way Mom is looking at me it's not happening.

"Let's talk in the den," Mom says. Perfect. I can hear in the den. I know it's "none of my business salad," but what if I'm in trouble about something? Why else would Tera's mom want to talk to Mom? I walk to the other side of the den where the piano is and sit at the piano.

"I just wanted to apologize to you for the gift card and the note. When Tera came home and said Joanna said some hurtful things about her, I got upset because Tera was so upset and I told Tera I wanted her to give Joanna's gift back. I was going through a really difficult time, and I wasn't thinking clearly."

"Well, I appreciate you saying that. I know that the girls have had their ups and downs, but I think they've gotten things straightened out now," Mom says.

"Tera and Joanna were best friends and then—I don't know what happened, but I wanted to apologize and let you know that Joanna is always welcome at our house. Tera told me about what she's doing at school and I think it's such a wonderful thing. We will donate, and I've also told some people at the news station that I used to work for and they may be doing a story on it. A reporter is coming to the school to read to a class for the book fair, so hopefully they can do a piece on the clothing drive as well."

"Oh really? That would be so nice. I know Joanna would love that. She loves the spotlight," Mom says.

"I'm gonna get a few errands out of the way while Tera's at the party, but I just wanted to come and apologize."

"Well, it was a pleasure meeting you and I'm sure we'll talk more as the girls stay in school together," Mom says.

"Well, Tera may be going to live with her father, I don't know yet—things are a little chaotic right now, but hopefully she'll be able to keep in touch and they can get together."

"Sounds good, and I hope things get better, it's definitely something I'll be praying about," Mom says.

"Thank you so much," Tera's mom says. I speed walk to the living room and find a plant to hide behind.

"I guess Tera thought I already left," Tera's mom says, looking around for Tera.

"Yeah, she's probably out there getting something to eat," Mom says.

What! They're eating without me?

"And what are you doing?" Mom says as Tera's mom closes the front door.

"Nothing." I bite my nails.

"If being nosy is nothing, then I guess you've got that covered," Mom says.

"What?" I put my hands on my hips.

"See? Everybody's outside eating while you're in here being nosy rosy," Mom says.

"I'm going to go eat now." I tiptoe away.

"Just make sure there's no gossip steak on that plate," Mom adds.

Everyone is sitting around the pool listening to music and eating hamburgers, hot dogs, and chips together.

"Mr. Earl? Can I have a hamburger please?" I ask.

"Of course you can, did you wash your front feet?" he asks, looking at my hands.

"My hands don't look anything like my feet," I laugh.

"You don't think so?" He looks at my hands. "I don't know, they look a little like feet to me."

"Leave that child alone and give her a hamburger. She's been asking for one all morning," Ms. Karyn says, rescuing me. Mr. Earl's grilled hamburgers are the best. My taste buds are lovin' it.

"I love your decorations," Tera says to Megan.

"Thanks," Megan smiles.

"We should have a water balloon fight," Lilia says.

"Let's have one in the pool," Kiara says. Mr. Earls throws all of the balloons in the pool and I pick up the biggest red balloon.

"Let the games begin," I say in my Dr. Boom voice. I throw the first balloon.

Memory Verse 26

1 John 3:18

"My children, our love should not be only words and talk.
No, our love must be real. We must show our love by the
things we do."

Today is the first day of the clothing drive and even the sun is excited; it's smiling down as I walk to the blacktop. I can't believe how many kids have brought sweaters and coats. Two boys walking in front of me have bags filled with coats and even teachers are carrying sweaters and coats from the parking lot.

"Look!" I point to the bins in front of the school. They are piling up with sweaters and coats. Mr. Suarez is standing next to the bins with a gigantic smile on his face. I brought two jackets and two sweaters to donate. Ms. Stacy, Megan, and I walk over to the donation bins.

"Good morning," Mr. Suarez says.

"Good morning, Mr. Suarez," Megan and I say at the same time.

"It's a nice turnout," Ms. Stacy says to Mr. Suarez.

"I was just talking with my Vice-Principal about that. I didn't think we had enough time to get the word out with the parent letters going out on Friday," Mr. Suarez says.

"Kids know how to spread the word," Ms. Stacy says.

"Absolutely, it's great." Mr. Suarez looks at me. As

we're standing here, so many kids are bringing sweaters.

"Hi Joanna," a fifth-grader says. I don't even know her name, but she knows my name.

"Who's that?" Megan asks.

"I don't know."

"What's up, Joanna," another kid I don't know says.

"Hey," I wave.

"You're popular now," Megan grins.

"No I'm not," I say, because like Mom says, I don't want to make it about me. It's about helping kids and stopping bullying.

"Yes you are, everybody knows you now," she says.

"Everybody wants the bullying to stop at our school," I answer.

"Hey Tera," I say as Tera lines up with us.

"Did you bring a sweater or a coat?" Megan asks.

"My mom collected sweaters and coats from everybody at her old job and she brought fifty-three coats and sweaters," Tera says.

"Fifty-three?" I ask.

"Yup," she says. Wow, I can't believe it.

"It's supposed to be for the kids who are being bullied and want the bullying to stop," Megan says.

"I *do* want bullying to stop," Tera says. Megan and Riley look at each other, but they don't say anything.

"Thank you for helping," I say to Tera.

"No problem," Tera mumbles.

In class, instead of doing our math warm-ups Mrs. Washington shows us a video about the different forms of bullying and there's a part where a girl makes fun of another girl and then says she's "just kidding."

"What does bullying mean to you?" Mrs. Washington asks. She draws brainstorm bubbles on the smartboard. Nobody raises a hand.

"Nobody has any thoughts about bullying? That really surprises me because everyone brought a sweater or a coat this morning," she says. Rachel raises her hand and everyone stares at her because normally she never raises her hand.

"Bullying means making a choice to hurt someone else on purpose," Rachel says. Mrs. Washington writes Rachel's thoughts in a brainstorm bubble.

"Okay, good, anybody else?" Tera raises her hand.

"Hitting someone," she says.

"Okay, so physically attacking someone," Mrs. Washington says, writing Tera's thoughts into a bubble. Evan raises his hand.

"Calling someone names," he says.

"Being verbally abusive, thank you, Evan. Do you all feel that bullying happens one time or is it something that happens more than once?" Mrs. Washington asks. Everyone agrees that it's more than once.

"Can it be spreading rumors about someone? Or making a hurtful meme about someone and texting it or posting it online or cyberbullying by saying mean things through social media websites?" Mrs. Washington asks.

"Yeah," I say, joining the rest of my class.

"What about telling your friends to ignore someone or leaving someone out of the group, can that be bullying too?"

Mrs. Washington asks. The class is quiet and I know why.

"I want you guys to get in your reading groups and make your own brainstorm bubbles. Think about why it's harder to recognize some forms of bullying and discuss it in your groups." Rachel is in my reading group and so are Tera, Javari, and Dominic.

"I think bullying is when someone steals your lunch money," Dominic says.

"That only happens on TV," Tera says.

"No it doesn't, it happened to my brother," Dominic says.

"I think it's when kids are in a circle whispering about you and pointing at you," I say.

"Yeah, because nobody can really tell it's bullying except you," Rachel says.

"People can tell, but it's hard to prove it," Javari says. Rachel and I both nod our heads.

"Especially to your parents. My mom always told me to ignore it, but sometimes you can't," Rachel says.

"What can your parents do about it?" Dominic asks.

"They can talk to the principal or the teacher," I say.

"*If* they believe you," Rachel says. "My mom always thinks I don't get along with anyone."

"Even if they do believe you, they can't make it stop," Dominic says.

"No, that's why you have to speak up," I say. Didn't they remember anything I said at the assembly?

"Nobody likes a rat," Dominic says.

"It's not being a rat. If you don't speak up then nobody

will know what's going on and it will only get worse. That's why we're doing the clothing drive, Dominic." I feel my cheeks get hot.

"I don't think it will help, because some kids don't care if they get in trouble. I don't," Dominic says.

"It will help if everybody does it," Rachel says.

"I don't think so, because even if you do tell, nothing happens. You can't force somebody to change," Dominic says.

"If you don't tell nothing happens either. Nobody deserves to be treated like that," I say. Mrs. Washington is at our table.

"I want you to stay on task. Why is it sometimes hard to recognize bullying?"

"Because kids are afraid to speak up," I say.

"Write your ideas down in your thought bubbles," Mrs. Washington says.

"Some kids are good at hiding it," Dominic says.

"But you can stick up for kids," I say.

"I always stick up for kids, but I'm not going to tell the teacher because I'm not a rat," Dominic says.

"I hope you got some ideas in your thought bubbles because we're going to share them," Mrs. Washington says. I wonder why Dominic brought a coat but still doesn't want to speak up. Why did he bring a coat if he thinks telling someone makes him a rat?

Lunchtime doesn't feel any better because Tera and Rachel are still not sitting with Megan, Riley, and Lilia even after Megan's party.

"I thought we were all friends," I say to Megan.

"Huh?" Megan asks taking a bite of her cookie.

"How come you don't want to sit with Tera and Rachel?" I ask.

"Because they didn't sit with us. We don't have to sit with them every single day, Joanna," Megan says.

"I know right? Just 'cause we're not sitting with them doesn't mean we're bullying them," Riley says.

"That's not what I meant," I mumble.

I don't know who I'm going to sit with. If I sit with Megan, Lilia, and Riley, then Tera and Rachel will think I don't want to sit with them.

"You can sit with them if you want," Megan says, reading my thoughts. I look at Tera and Rachel. They seem fine without me. They're laughing and they don't seem to notice that I'm not sitting with them.

"I'll stay here," I say.

"Did you see the clothing bins? They're all filled to the top," Lilia says.

"Yeah," I groan.

"Why are you sad?" Lilia asks.

"I'm not sad. I just thought things were going to be different." I put away my peanut butter and jelly sandwich.

"Different how?" Lilia asks.

"I thought things were going to change a lot more," I say.

"It's literally been one day, Joanna, what were you expecting?" Megan laughs.

"Plus, you can't change everybody," Lilia says. Maybe

she should sit with Dominic.

"You can only change yourself," Megan adds. I take a sip of my chocolate milk and try to follow Mom's advice to focus on the positive.

Memory Verse 27

Psalm 139:17
"Your thoughts are beyond my understanding.
They cannot be measured!"

It's 9:00 a.m. and nobody woke me up. We're supposed to be at the church to volunteer. Running down the stairs, I can hear everybody is already up.

"Good morning, sunshine," Ms. Karyn says.

"Aren't we late for volunteering?" I stare at the piles of suitcases in the middle of the living room.

"I thought I'd let you sleep in this morning," Mom carries her suitcase to the front door.

Megan is sitting on the couch with a big smile on her face she's up to something.

"Wanna play a game?" Megan laughs, looking at Mom. Mom smiles and so does Ms. Karyn.

"Um…okay," I rub my eyes.

"It's called…" Megan laughs. "We're going on a trip," she says. I look at Mom and she shrugs her shoulders.

"I know how to play." I fold my arms across my chest.

"You go first," Megan says.

"I'm going on a trip and I'm taking an apple," I say, sitting on the couch next to Megan. Mr. Earl and the boys are carrying the suitcases outside.

"An apple? No animal?" Mom says.

"What's going on? Are we going somewhere?" I scratch my right eyebrow.

"Can I play?" Mom sits down next to me.

"Sure," Megan giggles.

"What's so funny?" I ask.

"Your mom's turn," Megan says, ignoring my question.

"I'm going on a trip and I'm taking a beach," Mom says.

"Mom, you can't take a whole beach," I sigh.

"Yes she can," Megan says.

"See? Megan says I can," Mom says.

"You can't take a whole beach," I say.

"Alright, I won't take the whole beach. I'll just visit," Mom says. My heart is beating fast. Megan is laughing hysterically.

"We're going to the beach!" Megan shrieks.

"Seriously?" I jump on the couch cushion.

"We wanted to surprise you," Mom gives me a side hug.

"Yesssss!" I say dancing. "Oh yeah, oh yeah, going to the beach."

"Eat breakfast, we're leaving in an hour," Mom says. It's weird sitting at the big table by myself in my teddy bear pajamas.

"Ms. Jessica asked me to give this to you." Ms. Karyn hands me a pink envelope.

"What is it?"

"I don't know—she didn't say," Ms. Karyn places a plate of scrambled eggs, biscuit, and sausage links in front of me.

"Thank you." I take the envelope. Megan sits next to me as I open it. It's a card with a big red heart on the front with cursive letters that say "Thank you." On the inside it says:

Dear Joanna,

You don't know me, but we go to the same school, and I'm in third grade. I see you sometimes at church, but you don't see me because I'm with the 3rd graders and you're with the 5th graders.

I want to say thank you for what you did at our school. Some kids at our school were being really mean to me until we had the sweater and coat drive. I told my mom about what you did at our school and she told me that you help her at church. Thank you so much for stopping bullying at our school. I pray for you every day and I hope that you keep up the good work! It really means a lot to me.

Love,

Isabella

"What does it say?" Megan asks. I hand her the card so she can read it.

"See? You did make a difference." Megan gives me the card back. I hold it close to my heart. God had a plan the whole time and it was totally awesome. I just didn't see it until now.

Acknowledgments

I thank God for guiding me to all the right people. Thank you so much Lisa J. Amstutz I am truly grateful for your wisdom and guidance. Thank you to Qamber Kids and the talented Danielle Styles for bringing my vision to life. Thank you to Makeready Designs I appreciate you! Thank you to CookieLynn Publishing services and awesome Cassie Mae. Thank you to all the readers and supporters of this book, know that God created you on purpose, with purpose, for a purpose, God bless you.

Discussion Questions

1. What is your favorite memory verse or quote in the book?

2. Can someone be a bully without meaning to be? Why or why not?

3. Who can you talk to if someone is bullying you?

4. What is an important lesson everyone needs to know that you learned in the book?

5. Why do you think it's important to talk about your feelings instead of having a "Hoover Dam" like Joanna did?

6. When you see bullying, what can you do?

7. What advice would you give to someone who is afraid to speak up?

8. How do you feel friends treat each other?

9. Why do you think Tera felt betrayed?

10. Why do you think Joanna felt Megan changed? Do you feel Megan had a "Hoover Dam" why or why not?

About the Author

Amber Malone grew up in Riverside, California and now lives in Las Vegas, Nevada. When she's not writing, she spends a lot of time talking about why it's important to be kind to others. You might find her at Comic-Con dressed up as one of her favorite characters or skating backwards at a skating rink with her family.

You may email her at **sweatergirlsbook@gmail.com**